I0521219

The Empty Bar

By Edward S. Tonry

Copyright © 2018 Edward S. Tonry All rights reserved.

DEDICATION

This book is dedicated to Winifred Halsey,

who told me "Go ahead, give it a shot."

Cover by Judy Bullard

ISBN-13: 978-1-7326648-1-4

This is a work of fiction. Names, characters, businesses, places, events, locales, and incidents are either the products of the author's imagination or used in a fictitious manner. Any resemblance to actual persons, living or dead, or actual events is purely coincidental.

Unkempt Wombat Press

Chapter One

There was no one in the bar. He thought, *That's a bit unusual for four in the afternoon. It is a little early for happy hour, but surely someone should be having a drink. Getting ready for a late night at the office, done with shopping and ready to go home, celebrating a big sale – doesn't anybody have an excuse to wet his whistle?*

No one in the bar at all. No patrons. No waitress. No barman. No one. He could barely understand no patrons, but where were the staff? *Somebody should be here, waiting for a customer to show up. Somebody should be asking me "What'll you have?"* He looked behind the counter, and saw an open cash register, full of money, and nothing else. No barman asleep on the floor, or lying bleeding from a bashed in head. Nothing.

It was quiet. No sounds at all. No television showing highlights of last night's game. No radio sports talk show. No juke box playing oldies. No idle chatter. *I've never been in a quiet bar. This is unnerving. What the hell is going on?*

He turned back to the door, and looked at the sign: "Nick's Tavern. Open 12 noon to 2 am. Happy Hour 5 to 6." *OK, they were open, but empty.* He went back in, thought about the cash register, and closed the door, turning the deadbolt.

His ID said he was John Smith today. A convenient name for today's planned activities, but it might become awkward. *If there is really no one here, I'll have to call the police. They won't like that name, it sounds like I'm trying to hide something. Still, whatever has happened does not involve me. They will ask me a few questions and I'll be on my way, with my own questions.*

He turned back into the bar and looked it over closely. He hadn't bothered to check it out when he came in. Why should he, it was just a bar. But now it was an empty bar, something that wasn't right. *Is there some obvious reason that a normal bar should become an empty bar? There's no smell of smoke in the air, so there wasn't a fire. And if there had been, there would be firemen, and the staff would be out on the sidewalk. There's also no smell of gunpowder, so there's been no shooting.*

It was a standard tavern, maybe twenty-five feet wide, and probably fifty or sixty feet deep. The only variation he ever saw in these old style bars was that sometimes the owners ran two storefronts together to make a bigger place. The bar counter was only ten feet long, making more space for a couple of extra tables. The tables were square with clean blue tablecloths, and spaced comfortably apart. No one was going to be bumping into anyone else. *Fewer tables meant fewer customers, too. But none? Hardly.*

The floor was linoleum, worn, but clean, with a bland, fake stone pattern. The walls were covered with a pale green wallpaper with a vague pattern in it. This bar was nothing fancy, but it was clean and fairly respectable looking. And it was just down 26th Street from Berwyn's city offices. *Does the city hire only teetotalers? This place should have customers by late afternoon. Where are they?*

In the back were the toilets. He went into the men's room and found it as empty as the bar. He looked at his reflection in the mirror and grimaced. *I'm starting to get too old for adventures, and this is beginning to look like an adventure.* He was still short of fifty years old, but not that short any more. His hair was still a nice soft brown, not yet turning gray. He wore a decent light blue suit today, but not too nice. It sat on his five foot, ten inch frame as if it had been tailored just for him, which it had been. *I've got to start working out again, the suit is getting tight. I was 180 pounds today, got to get back to 170. Time to start doing some exercise. Tomorrow. Next week. That can wait. What else is wrong here now?*

He went to the women's room and hesitated. He knocked on the door, shouted out "Is anyone in there?," and knocked again. Still hesitating, he pushed the door open and stepped in. Three stalls, all empty. Not a trace of any one using this toilet, either. Same glum guy looking back from the mirror.

The office was across from the toilets, its door wide open. The glass covering a framed business license behind the desk reflected a shelf over the door. On it stood four surveillance camera screens facing the desk. One showed the open door from the street, another the barman behind the bar, wiping a glass. He poked his head out of the office and looked down the bar. The front door was still closed, and no one was still behind the bar.

The office was small and the desk took up a large part of the floor. There were shelves on two walls lined with phone books and catalogs from the people who supplied taverns with everything they needed. A closed filing cabinet stood in the corner by the door, and a small fan sat on top, pointing toward the desk. The wallpaper here was yellow, and looked years older than the paper in the main room. *One way to save a little money,* he thought.

A computer monitor on the desk showed a spreadsheet listing invoices. A half-filled glass with a single small ice cube sat next to the mouse. An I-phone lay face down on the desktop. There was a small safe behind the desk. Its door was open and a shelf held a moderate stack of bills. No one here, either. No sign of anyone having been here, except the half-filled glass and the open safe.

The back door was closed firmly. When he opened it, he saw that there was no knob on the outside, just a keyhole and a small handle to grab and pull. There was nobody there, either, just an empty alley. There was a dumpster beside the door with a few flattened cardboard boxes inside. There were other dumpsters and trash cans up and down the alley, but no people.

Inside, beside the back door, were stairs going down into the cellar. He followed them down to a very ordinary tavern basement. Cases of booze, barrels of beer, boxes of napkins, cocktail toothpicks, olives, toilet paper, everything a bar might need. Except people.

He walked around the piles, looking for someone unconscious, drunk, dead, anything. Not a soul. Nothing disturbed, nothing askew, nothing on the floor. No blood stains, no spilled beer or liquor. Nothing. He felt he was on a movie set, and the cast hadn't yet showed up.

He went back up to the bar and used his own phone to call 911.

"Nine one one, what is your emergency?" asked the operator.

"I'm in Nick's Tavern on 26th Street, in Berwyn, and the place is deserted," he said.

"Deserted?" asked the operator, "what do you mean by 'deserted'?"

"Deserted," he repeated, "there's no one here. No bartender. No one. There's money in the till, and no owner or barman or anyone. Could you please send a squad over to check it out?"

He unlocked and opened the front door, and then stood in it. It was a nice day, sunny and warm for late September. *A nice day for a nice cool beer. I wish I could get one, but if I help myself, the police will say I contaminated the scene. Phooey.* He had to shoo off a couple of guys looking for an early drink, and then the police arrived.

Two uniformed policemen got out of the squad and walked up to the door.

"You the guy who called?" asked the taller man. He was about thirty or a little bit over, with short dish-water blond hair and three stripes on his sleeve. His partner was younger, mid-twenties, black haired and looked eager for something to work on.

"Yeah, my name's John Smith. Yes, John Smith. Don't look at me like that, I get that all the time. Here's my driver's license. It's not my fault that my parents were not very imaginative."

"I'm Sergeant Doyle, and this is Patrolman Saunders. What's going on here? They just told us there was no one in a bar. Is that a crime now?"

"No, but it's not right, either," said Smith. "I visit bars regularly, not too much, but regularly, and I've never seen an empty bar at four in the afternoon. And not just no customers, there's nobody here at all. No barman, no waitress, no manager. The cash register and the office safe are standing open, and still full of money. I can't figure it out, so I thought I'd share the mystery with you boys."

Sergeant Doyle gestured Smith back into the bar, and the two policemen made the same search Smith had already done. Smith sat down at a table and waited for them to finish. They didn't bother knocking on the women's room door, but their search still took longer.

"Nothing in the cellar, either," said Saunders, topping the stairs. "No signs of scuffles or disturbance down there, any more than up here."

"The only signs that anyone but you has been here all day," said Doyle, "are the open cash register, the open safe, and a half-filled glass of something."

"With a small ice cube in it," added Smith.

"There's no ice in it now," said Doyle. "How long ago did you come in here?"

"I got here just about four o'clock," said Smith. "It probably took me about five or six minutes to make my way to the office. That would be about half an hour ago," checking his watch.

"Really?" said Doyle. "When you came up the street, did you see anyone coming out of this bar?"

"No, but the ice cube could have been melting for a while when I saw it," said Smith. "And someone could have gone out the back door. I tried it, and it's not locked from the inside."

"All right," said Doyle. "Just keep seated and get comfy. I've called for some detectives from downtown to take over. We're just street cops. When they want puzzles solved, they get the guys in suits to do it. In the meantime, because they'll want to know, I'm going to need to know your address, phone number, place of employment, and why you came in here."

"Here's my business card, it has most of that information," said Smith. "I came in here because I was thirsty. I've been doing things all day, and thought a beer would be a very nice way to end the afternoon."

"It usually is. I wish we could get one now," said Saunders, "but it'll be eight before we're off duty."

"Yeah, it's a hard life, Saunders," said a voice from the door. "At least you work a fairly fixed shift. A detective has to work until the case is solved, even if it takes years. No sleep, no days off, just work, work, work."

"Right, Mahoney," said Saunders, laughing at an old in-joke. "I do appreciate the difference in our hours. I would gladly trade my hours for your pay. Deal? Didn't think so."

A woman followed Mahoney into the bar, and Sergeant Doyle filled the two detectives in on what Smith had told him, and what they had seen. The detectives looked at Smith as Doyle talked. He looked back at them.

Mahoney was pushing fifty, with a little gray mixed into the black at his temples. but he had a bright, searching eye, looking at everything in the large bar room. He wore a wrinkled brown suit, and his tie was loose at the collar. He was probably five feet eight, and one seventy five pounds. He had a small pot belly, but his back was ramrod straight, and he carried himself well. He had the light walk of a man who knew how to fight if he had to, and who thought he would win if he fought.

The woman was younger, maybe thirty, with medium length brunette hair. She wore a skirt, blouse, and a short jacket that almost matched the skirt. *No purse, must have left it in the car. All business*, he thought. She was attractive, but not enough to make him rehearse his pick-up lines. She was short, about five feet five, and maybe a hundred thirty pounds. She looked and acted competent, capable. Unlike Mahoney, her capabilities were not obvious, but Smith knew she was very good at something. There had to be some reason for that air of confidence.

Doyle and Saunders made their way out of the bar, and the two detectives came over to the table where Smith was waiting.

"I'm Detective Mahoney, and this is Detective Inspector Radcliffe. Yeah, the young kid bosses the old guy around. That's because she's smarter than I am. And I'm not dumb."

"OK, I get it," said Smith, "you have the experience to see clues, she has the talent to see clues, and here you are where there aren't many clues at all. Do you want me to go over what Sergeant Doyle already told you? Or have you already got some new questions for me?"

"First question," said Radcliffe, "your card gives your occupation as 'Services.' Just what kind of 'services' do you provide, and to whom?"

"Ah, good question, good grammar," said Smith. "I do favors for people. Take today, for instance. A man who has a fair amount of money, but no people working for him to do special, personal, favors, gave me three envelopes. One is to pay the rent on the apartment of his mistress. One is to pay the mistress her monthly spending money. The third envelope is my fee for delivering the other two envelopes.

"He doesn't want to use checks, because checks have names on them, and can be traced. And he doesn't want his wife to find out about the mistress, naturally. So I run the errands for him, for a fee. I know many men like him. They don't all have mistresses, but they all have errands to run which would be embarrassing for them to run.

"I sometimes skirt the edge of the line of the law, but I don't think I've ever crossed over it. It would be more profitable to cross that line, but more dangerous, too. I don't deliver drugs, or drug money. It is possible some of my employers may be, or have been, in the drug business, but my errands are legitimate, fairly legal, even if sometimes immoral. Next question."

"Interesting," said Mahoney, "are you a lawyer? Or do you work for a lawyer?"

"No," said Smith, "a lawyer would ask for more money than I do, and have a more observable connection to the client. That really answers both of your questions. I do often get recommended by lawyers, as well as by word of mouth. But I don't work for anyone but myself, and my clients."

"So, you're just a bagman," said Mahoney, with disgust.

"What other kinds of errands do you run?" asked Radcliffe, simultaneously.

"Placing bets with bookies, collecting on the winning bets, arranging girls for guys who can't afford to keep a mistress. I don't really care for the term 'bagman'. I'm an errand boy, a go-between, a non-political fixer. I'll take a politician's daughter to the abortion clinic on the sly. I'll take his wife to the addiction clinic, also on the sly. There are all kinds of jobs that people with money want done, but don't want to do themselves. I live on other people's fear of embarrassment."

"Well, I can't see how that matters here," said Mahoney. "You said you didn't touch anything, Did you notice anything unusual while you were looking around?"

"Only the surveillance monitors," said Smith. "They showed the front door open, after I had closed it. And they showed the barman polishing a glass. I looked again, and there was still no one there."

"You've got a good eye," said Radcliffe. "Those monitors are still showing the same scenes. Have you ever been in this bar before?"

"No, I had finished my errands, and was walking toward the bus stop. I wanted a beer, the bar was here, I went in."

"You have a driver's license, and yet you take the bus. Why?" asked Mahoney.

"Have you ever tried to park in this part of town? Of course not, you've got a squad, and a special 'I'm a cop' card for your non-squad car, so you can park anywhere you want. I have an easy job, one that doesn't normally take a lot of my time. But I still don't want to waste my free time looking for a parking space."

"The cash register is open, the safe is open," said Mahoney, "may we see the contents of your pockets? Please."

"I wondered when that question was going to come up," said Smith. "Here you go: one wallet, with $22 in it, a key ring, a Swiss army knife, a few coins, a handkerchief, my phone, an envelope with my fee, still sealed. You may open it if you want, and, unless he cheated me, or gave me a raise, you will find thirteen hundred dollar bills."

"That's not a bad day's pay for half a day's fixing," jeered Mahoney.

"No, that's what I made for today's errand," said Smith. "I charge 10% of the amount for cash transfers. And it's a job I would normally do next Monday, the first. Today's client is going out of town, and wanted the errand run today. Next Monday I have three more clients, so I will make more, a lot more. They all have greedier mistresses."

"Just double checking," said Mahoney, "you say you got here about when?"

"About four o'clock," said Smith. "I looked around the place to see if anyone was here, and called 911 about ten or fifteen minutes later. I could have called right away, but I wanted to check the basement. If someone was down there, hurt, I would have asked for an ambulance, too."

"Very decent of you, Mr. Smith," said Radcliffe. "Any more questions you can think of, Sam?"

"No, it's easy to finish questioning a witness who didn't see anything," said Mahoney.

"All right, thank you for your time," said Radcliffe. "I don't think we need anything more from you now. Let us know if you are leaving town for any time, just in case we come up with any more questions. But I think this is likely the last time you'll see us. Thanks, again."

Smith left the bar and walked down the street. He stopped in front of a shop and looked into the display window. Out of the corner of his eye, he checked the street behind him. No one was following him. He smiled, went around the corner, and got into his car. He put his wallet into the glove box, took another wallet from it, and Mr. John Smith disappeared. Mr. Jack Sorenson put the car in gear, and drove off.

***

Where the hell was Peterson? he thought as he worked through the early evening traffic. *He said he would be there by four at the latest. And, given his insistence on punctuality, he should have been there ten minutes earlier, if not more. Is he missing, too? Is he why everyone there is missing?*

There was no disturbance. The police confirmed that. No one was likely to take Peterson for a walk without obvious signs of a disturbance. And he didn't think Peterson was likely to be involved in anything that could turn violent. I'll have to call him when I get home. Or maybe drop a note at his hidey-hole. Both, it won't hurt.

***

Peterson called it his hidey-hole, but he got the idea from reading spy novels. Despite his rather prosaic occupation as a fixer and go-between, he was a romantic. He wanted a more glamorous life than he had. He was paid well, but there was no drama, no adventure, no excitement. He liked to think of himself as some sort of non-governmental secret agent. Spies used dead drops, or dead letter boxes. Peterson, knowing how popular spy novels were and not wanting to use a common term, called his a hidey-hole.

The reality was less romantic. There was a bench in the park near his apartment, with a small hole under the seat, where a piece of wood had been chipped out. Peterson had found the hole by accident, realized its possibilities, and used it for passing indiscreet messages. He checked it regularly, but usually found nothing. He did sometimes use it to leave messages for others. They shook their heads in amusement, but went along with the gag.

There was no need to leave him a message today, however. Peterson was sitting on the bench, watching a couple of squirrels race around the park. It was late September, but rather warm, and he didn't try to hide his balding head under a cap. He was wearing a green checked short-sleeved shirt and a pair of faded jeans, and he had a folded newspaper in his hand.

His round, plump face was wrinkled with too many summers outdoors, and too many evenings in bars. He claimed to be sixty, to justify the wrinkles, but the last ten years was just padding.

Sorenson walked casually from his car into the park, said a few polite words to a woman with a baby carriage and a calico cat, and took a drink of water from a fountain at the center of the park. Having thus checked out the entire area, and being satisfied no one was paying him or Peterson any attention, he sat down on the bench, two feet from Peterson.

"I've never known you not to show up on time," said Sorenson quietly. "Being where you say you'll be and punctuality are your trademarks. What happened? The bar was empty and I wound up calling the police. I only did that because I was afraid something might have happened to you."

"You know me well enough to know that if something happens to me, there'll be signs of it," said Peterson. "I knew you would expect me, that was the whole plan. I wanted you to call the cops. I spent a lot of time and effort to make sure those two detectives would show up to investigate. I wanted the broad to meet you, and you to meet her."

"Opening up a dating service?" asked Sorenson, sarcastically. "She's nice looking, but not enough to make my pulse race. What's the real deal?"

"Okay, here's what's happening," said Peterson. "I needed a way for you and the female detective to meet. So I put on a Halloween mask, grabbed an unloaded shotgun, and went into the bar. You know I don't like shooting, but nobody argues with a shotgun, and nobody wants to find out if it's loaded or not. I had a van parked in the alley behind the place, and just marched the bartender, the waitress, and the boss out the back door and into the van.

"I took them to the old gravel quarry by the river, you know the place we used to hang out at, and left them in the shack. It's still there, but more dilapidated than ever. You are going to be the big hero and help rescue them. Actually, the cops are going to be pissed at you for not telling them about your meeting with me, and the delay in finding the people. But they can't tie you into the kidnapping, 'cause you didn't know about it until now.

"Anyway, the broad's shift is over at eight tonight. About seven, I want you to call her up, or drop in at the station, doesn't matter, and tell her you now know where the missing people are. Take her out to the gravel pit, find the folks, everybody goes back to the station house and talks for a few hours. You'll get to do more talking than they will, but that's what you're getting paid for.

"Don't mention my name, or our supposed meeting, if you can avoid it. And I think you can. Just say you got a call from some anonymous person, telling you where the victims are. I'm not concerned about being identified because of the mask – I chose one as unlike my face as possible.

"Here's the important part. You have to keep Radcliffe occupied until at least two in the morning. Stall her interrogation. If you can't, then take her out to dinner because you kept her busy so late. Take her out for a drink. Take her to bed. Maybe your pulse will race if she's naked. Just keep her from going home until at least two o'clock.

"For your inconvenience, there's fifteen large in an envelope inside this newspaper. I'll leave it here on the bench when I get up in a minute. Any questions?"

"What for?" said Sorenson, glumly. "The only answer you'll give me is 'fifteen large' – I know the routine. I have a bad feeling about this, Pete. I don't suppose I can turn it down?"

"I don't like it either," said Peterson, "and I know more about it than you do. But I don't think either of us is going to get hurt by the deal, or get in any serious trouble. I have to worry about the kidnapping, but I don't think they'll tag that one on me. The rest should be just a mystery to everyone, and one they'll forget after a while. In any case, you are out of it after two o'clock.

"Look, I picked you because I know you, and your abilities. Everybody thinks George Clooney is the ultimate suave, smooth-talking charmer in the movies. You could give him lessons. You can sweet talk a nun out of her knickers. You can take the heat better, and more calmly, than anyone I know. You haven't done anything wrong, and can't be charged with anything. Hell, even if they should catch me for the kidnapping, you weren't in on that."

"All right," said Sorenson, resigned to his fate, "I'll visit Inspector Radcliffe at seven tonight, and keep her out till the cows come home.

What I'll do for money. And her partner was ragging me for making so much for my morning's work. If he only knew what I made for overtime."

***

The bank advertised itself as the "Friendly Bank" and tried to make that honest advertising by keeping longer hours than most banks. It was after six o'clock before Sorenson arrived, but the lobby was still open, and so was the vault. He put most of the $15,000 from Peterson in his safe deposit box. Three hundred from his first envelope went into his wallet. Upstairs a teller gave him a smiling greeting, and the other thousand, and two more from Peterson's envelope, went into his bank account. Two minutes later, with his money safely deposited, and a receipt in his pocket, Sorenson went across the street for an early dinner. Seven o'clock was coming on fast and he knew it would be a long time before he had another chance to eat.

Chapter Two

"My name is Mr. John Smith, and I'd like to talk to Detective Inspector Radcliffe, please. It's about a case she handled this afternoon. I have some new information for her."

The desk sergeant gave him the fish eye at his name, but changed his face when he heard Radcliffe's name mentioned. He picked up a phone and punched an internal number.

"She'll be out in a minute. Take a seat on that bench," he told Smith.

"Ah, the unusual Mr. John Smith," said Radcliffe, entering the lobby. "You exist again. Did you know that you don't seem to live where you say you live? Why don't you follow me back to my office. I need to have a much more serious talk with you."

"Of course, I'll be happy to tell you anything you like," lied Smith, "but first you should hear why I'm here now. I got a phone call from someone, saying the people missing from the bar are at an old gravel pit south of town, near the canal. Maybe you'd like to rescue them."

"A call from whom? And why didn't you call us immediately?" demanded Radcliffe.

"The caller didn't identify herself, but she had a high-pitched voice. And I thought you'd want me to take you to the pit. There's a special pit there we used to hang out in when I was in high school. It's not near the other pits in the quarry. I guess she used to hang out there, too."

"Hmmm, maybe I'll buy that," said Radcliffe, skeptically. "George, get a squad ready to come with us, and keep an eye on this fellow while I get Mahoney."

***

Ten minutes later Smith was sitting in the back of an unmarked car driven by Mahoney. A squad with two cops followed them out of town. Smith gave directions, more often than he had thought he would have to. Apparently the gravel quarry was no longer popular with the party crowd.

"Gravel pit" is a general name for a source of crushed rock, small stones, smaller stones, and sand. The proprietors use power shovels to dig the material out of the ground, making pits. Different types of small stones and sand may be present in the same ground, so a site may have several pits. The canal site mostly provided pea gravel, but it also had a pit full of very fine sand. Near the sand pit, stood a small wooden shack, leaning to one side and barely erect.

They pulled up by the decrepit shack, its door open, hanging by only one hinge at the top. The two cops went into the shack first, followed by the two detectives, and Smith took up the rear. Three people were inside, shackled by the leg to a post holding up the roof. They could stand and walk, but the chains were just long enough for them to reach a jug of water and a slop bucket. Their hands were not tied, their mouths not gagged.

A man whom Smith recognized from the surveillance tape as the bartender sat on one side of the post. He was maybe thirty-five, with dark hair, brown or black wasn't obvious in the dark shack. He wore a short-sleeved white shirt and dark slacks, and still had on his bar apron.

Next to him was the blonde waitress, wearing red pedal pushers and a V-necked short-sleeved yellow top. Smith hadn't thought the bar was quite that casual. She was forty, at least, not as slim as she'd like to be, but still good looking enough to make decent tips.

A very gloomy older man with a bad comb-over sat next to her. His black suit was crumpled and dirty, and not just from the place he was in. He gave the impression of a man who had never had a break, would never get a break, and, if anyone ever did give him a break, he'd lose it somehow.

They shouted with joy at seeing their rescuers, talking all at once and drowning each other's voices. The only discernible comment was a demand to be unshackled. The cops looked at the locks on the chains and said, "We don't have a key for these locks – it's not police standard."

"The key is over by the bathroom," said Smith.

"What bathroom?" asked the indignant waitress, "I had to use that slop bucket over there. At least the guys turned away and plugged their ears."

"Back when my high school friends would come out here," said Smith, "we used the lean-to next to this shack as a bathroom. We put an outhouse seat over a hole in the ground. The woman who called me said the key to the chains was there, and so are their phones."

One of the cops went out, and returned shortly with a bag and a key. He used the key to free the kidnap victims, and they pulled their cell phones from the bag.

"If you need to call someone to let them know you're OK," said Mahoney, "go ahead, but keep it short, and tell them you won't be home for a while, yet. We'll have to take you back to the station to get statements from all of you."

After explaining about the "bathroom," Smith had been quiet and unobtrusive. He watched what was happening, but not as if he was connected to it. He did not seem to be looking at anything or anyone in particular, but he did notice that Radcliffe was watching him closely. He pretended not to notice.

                                   ***

Back at the station house, Smith was taken to an interrogation room and shut in. The room was about ten feet long by eight feet wide, with a large table and four chairs. There was no clock, or anything else, on the walls. The cheap tile on the floor was scuffed, dirty, and broken in places. The wooden chairs were not designed with comfort in mind. It was a place to question people without being friendly about it. It was a place to sweat confessions out of criminals. It was a place to make reluctant witnesses uncomfortable enough to talk. Smith sat down, pulled Peterson's newspaper from his pocket, and waited.

The three bar employees were taken to a large room with a long table and several chairs. It was not as intimidating as the room Smith was in, but it was still institutional. It was a place for staff meetings, conferences, planning sessions before raids. There were a few small posters about police regulations and procedures on the walls, and the standard round office clock. One of the fluorescent lights flickered slightly.

A medic had been called in to give them a quick examination. While waiting for him to finish, Radcliffe had a patrolman run down the street to a burger joint, and get a bag of sandwiches for them. The medic checked all of them over quickly but found no signs of trauma, or injuries beyond the chafing of the shackles, or anything else but fright. So he packed up his gear, and allowed the detectives to interview them.

The bar employees all told the same story. A man in a light-weight topcoat and an Abraham Lincoln mask had walked into the bar a little before four o'clock. He looked around and pulled a shotgun out from under his topcoat. He told the bartender to open the cash register, and then walked him and the waitress toward the office in the back. The man had not touched the money in the register, hadn't even gone behind the bar.

In the office he made the manager open the safe and leave it open. He knew where the surveillance recorder was and went right over to it. He took the tape out of the machine and put it in his coat pocket, replacing it with another he had with him. He made them give him their cell phones, except the manager. He told the manager to leave his I-phone on the desk, logo side up. Then he marched all three of them out the back door, and told them to get into a panel van parked in the alley.

He fastened the chains on them there, and the other ends of the chains were attached to the frame of the van. He drove them away very carefully, trying to avoid potholes in the alley, and not speeding or running traffic lights. After some time he stopped and unlocked the chains from the van frame. He made them get out and go into the shack, where he attached the chains to the post. He showed them the water and the slop bucket, and told them someone would rescue them in a few hours.

They told their tales in turn, but it was all the same story, plus or minus personal gripes about the way they were treated. When they were all done, Radcliffe and Mahoney thanked them for their help, and left them with a uniformed cop to get their signatures on their statements before leaving.

"That's quite an interesting story," said Mahoney, "do you believe it?"

"Oh, of course," said Radcliffe, "why would anyone make up such a ridiculous story? Legally, they have been kidnapped. But no demands were made for their release, and the kidnapper, or his accomplice, apparently called in himself to get them released. The kidnapper, let's call him X, insisted that the cash register and the safe be opened, and then showed no further interest in them. He obviously wanted us to be mystified by that, but we can actually discount it as a ploy on his part."

"He had prepared the chains, the van, the water and bucket at the shack," said Mahoney. "So he was planning this for at least a few hours."

"Days," said Radcliffe. "He had a surveillance tape that ran a loop. He must have gotten hold of a real tape and done some splicing to make the loop. That would take some time."

"Showing off again" said Mahoney. "I hadn't spotted that yet. How did Smith know you have that talent?"

"You would have seen it, too," said Radcliffe, "but that brings us back to Smith. This interview was easy. I think Smith is going to be a challenge. Are you ready?"

***

Smith looked up from his newspaper when they came into the small room.   He had brought the paper because he knew he would be left alone for a long while. He had been interrogated before, always by suspicious policemen, and sometimes with justification. Interrogations were never short. They were sometimes unpleasant, too. He didn't think this one would be terribly unpleasant, but he might be wrong.

"So where do you really live?" said Mahoney, beginning the questioning as brusquely as possible. "We went to the address on your card to ask you some more questions, but you weren't home. In fact, the nosy lady next door informed us that you are rarely home. You mostly show up maybe once a week, always with a girl, and not often with the same girl. She disapproved of that. I'm just jealous.

"But if you don't live there, where do you live? And why give us a phony address? Did you think we would not check it out?"

"Like most of my clients I prefer to stay anonymous," said Smith. "They feel safer dealing with a man who also wants to be unknown. And if I have to do something for them that attracts attention, John Smith is the best name to give to anybody with an inquiring mind. This afternoon I saw no reason to give any other identification. I didn't know about the kidnapping then, though I thought it was a possibility. I didn't think I was going to have a larger role in this story.

"Here's my real ID," said Sorenson, "with my real address. You can send someone there now to check it out, if you want. I'll even give you a key and written permission to search the place. You won't find anything about this affair, or anything else."

"Nothing else at all?" asked Mahoney.

"Nothing else at all," said Sorenson.

"No client list, no records of moneys received," said Mahoney, "how do you prepare your income taxes without records of income?"

"I didn't say that was the only address I use," said Sorenson. "If I think you need to know more about me, or if you can get a warrant and force me, I'll give you some more addresses. Plural. I am a cautious man."

"So what was your role in this kidnapping?" asked Radcliffe, speaking for the first time. "We have figured out it was a fake, with enough red herrings to open a fish and chips shop. Why? What was your plan?"

"I told you, I just happened to walk into that bar," said Sorenson. "I had no idea anything was going to be different from any other time I've gone into a bar. If I had been a little earlier, I'd have been bundled off with the others. And I would have been a little bit earlier if the woman to whom I had been delivering her monthly payment hadn't wanted to talk my ear off with complaints about her lover boy. In fact, if I had just had the sense to see her first, and then drop the other envelope off at the landlord's office, I would have gone into some other bar."

"Wonderful story," said Radcliffe , "better than most I've heard over the years. Did you notice, Sam, how he diverted our attention from the red herrings to how he spent his day?"

"Who is Abraham Lincoln?" asked Mahoney .

"Fifteenth, sixteenth President of the United States?" replied Sorenson, uncertainly. "I'm not much of a history buff."

"Cute, Sorenson," said Mahoney, "but we don't want to hear your wise cracks. Who was wearing the Abe Lincoln mask?"

"What Abe Lincoln mask?" asked Sorenson, with a perplexed expression. "What are you talking about?"

"The guy who kidnapped those people was wearing an Abe Lincoln mask," said Mahoney. "Who was wearing it?"

"That's the first time you've said anything about a mask," said Sorenson. "How would I know what the kidnapper was wearing when he and they were all gone before I walked into the bar? I told you, if I had been there, I'd probably have been carted off as well. Do you think I can see the future? Do you think I said to myself, go into that bar and watch Abe Lincoln kidnap some people? How could I possibly know who was in a mask I haven't ever seen? And I'll swear to that."

"You could have known if you were in on the whole thing from the start," said Radcliffe. "You and some unknown partner staged this whole thing for some mysterious reason. Who was he, and what was the scheme?"

"I told you, I knew nothing about any kidnapping when I went into that bar," said Sorenson. "Yeah, looking around and finding nobody there, the possibility of a kidnapping did occur to me – that's why I called the police. Duh. But I didn't expect to find a kidnapping when I went in, just a cold beer. If someone is pulling your chain, it isn't me. Would I deliberately set myself up for a long night of interrogation from you two? If there was some gag here, why would I make myself the fall guy?"

"Let's talk," said Radcliffe to Mahoney, getting up from her chair.

Out in the corridor, she said, " He's clever. He hasn't admitted anything, and he doesn't really add anything to what he has already said. The first thing he said to me this afternoon was a compliment on my grammar. He is careful about what he says and how. His denials are very specific. He said ' I knew nothing about any kidnapping when I went into that bar' and that may be true. But it avoids saying what he knows about it now. He knows how to use words, including how to hide things in plain sight.

"But he's got a point. Why would he make himself the butt of this, if it was a joke? Why be the only one in a kidnapping plot to be picked up? And do it deliberately? Why was there a kidnapping? There was no demand for ransom, no money taken at the scene, no serious harm to the victims. As I said, under the law, it is still a kidnapping. But what was really happening? And why?"

"Damned if I know," said Mahoney. "I think he's hiding something, too. I think he knows all about this. But I can't figure out what 'this' is either. And I don't think we can hold him because we suspect his grammar. Give him a long leash and keep an eye on him?"

"That'll work for now," said Radcliffe. "It's getting late. The captain's not going to like this overtime on an imaginary kidnapping. We can get a warrant and go over to his real apartment tomorrow and see what's to be found there. I don't think we'll find anything, not with him admitting to multiple addresses. Put Markham on him, he's a good tail."

Sorenson was disappointed when he was released. It was just after twelve-thirty. He hadn't kept Inspector Radcliffe occupied long enough. He needed another hour and a half of her time.   He would have to try a different approach.

Chapter Three

Sorenson knew people who could help him. Lots of people in lots of places. A few of them were important, but most were nobodies, but nobodies who could help if they wanted. And most wanted to help if a few bucks came their way in exchange. And in exchange for a PayPal "gift", a guy he knew at the DMV had earlier given him the license plate number of Radcliffe's car. He was waiting next to it when she came out of the station.

"You are a very strange person," Radcliffe said in an even, controlled tone. "I'm not going to ask how you knew that is my car. It would only disappoint you to think I was dumb enough not to know. And why you wanted to know is also easy. But what I don't know is why you want to talk to me out here, and not inside. Don't you like Mahoney?"

"Detective Mahoney is a nice guy," said Sorenson with a smile, "and, as he said, he's not dumb. But I know Detective Mahoney. Not personally, I've never met him before. But I know him as a type, the solid, dependable detective who has seen everything and knows all the angles. I know him and how to handle him. And he knows me, from my prototypes, and how to handle me.

"But I don't know you, or your type, very well. You are a younger police woman, with a different training, maybe a different background. Police departments are changing all the time, new hiring practices, new training techniques. I'd like to find out how you differ from Detective Mahoney.

"I've only told you a small slice of what I do to make money. And in my line of work I need to know all about people, all kinds of people, including the police. It's not just how to trick them. It's more about how to work with or around them. Where are the real lines, not just the ones in the law books. What might they not really care about? Is this a crime in Cicero, but not in Berwyn? How do the police think? And why do they think that way?

"So I thought we might go out for a late meal, or a snack. A steak, a sandwich, a piece of mom's apple pie and a cup of coffee. I've kept you up pretty late, and ought to make it up to you." Another smile.

"I suppose you must have had a mother," said Radcliffe, "most people do. [sigh] It's too late to eat anything. I've been on the job since noon, and it's now past midnight. I just want to go to bed. Did she actually bake pies?"

"No," said Sorenson, "but she bought them from a really good bakery. How about a quick drink, then? A long day can always feel better after a stiff shot of something."

"No, not a drink, either," said Radcliffe. "This afternoon you were a witness to something odd. This evening you became, not a suspect, but a 'person of interest' in a kidnapping. I'm not quite sure what you are, but I do know that I shouldn't even be talking to you here in the parking lot."

"Would you like to come up to my place and see my etchings?" asked Sorenson, with a grin, ignoring her reason for brushing him off.

"Yes, you are odd enough, you might have etchings," said Radcliffe. "But, no, my husband wouldn't approve."

"Oh, I'm sorry," said Sorenson, "I didn't know you were married. I didn't see a ring."

"The stone came loose," said Radcliffe, "and it's at the jeweler's for repair. You also didn't see the mark where the ring normally sits. You're slipping. That's the first thing you missed today. At the gravel pit I noticed you watching me watching you.

"And a man who delivers payments to mistresses, and arranges women for those who can't afford mistresses, is too moral to seduce a married woman. How interesting."

"Not too moral, too interested in preserving my hide" said Sorenson, unbuttoning three buttons of his shirt and moving his tie. "Look at this."

Radcliffe looked at a small, round, white scar in the center of his chest. "Most people have their hearts at that spot. Are you one of those odd folks whose internal organs are out of place?"

"No, my heart's there, too," said Sorenson. "I was having a fun time with a blonde when her husband came home early. He went to the dresser for his gun. I grabbed my clothes and went out the door, slamming it behind me. I was pulling up my pants and turning to see if he was coming after me when he shot. The bullet went through the door and hit me dead center. Well, it would have been dead if it hadn't been a .22, and hadn't gone through a door. So, now I look for unmarried women to play with.

"So, you're married. That's fine. Marriage isn't for me, but I'm all in favor of it for other people. What does your husband do for a living?"

"He's a cop, too," said Radcliffe, "and he'll be here pretty soon, if you don't leave. He works Homicide, and his shift ends later than mine, but it's almost over now."

"Your husband's with the police, too?" said Sorenson. "That's fine. It's always nice to have someone who understands your work to talk to about it."

"Hmmmm. I just noticed something about the way you talk," said Radcliffe. "Most people say 'cop.' Even I just did. But every time I've heard you talk about cops, you've said 'police' instead. The only time you said 'cop' was that joke about the 'I'm a cop' card. I told Mahoney you were very careful about your language, and I keep being surprised by just how careful you are."

"So, let's all go out for a drink," said Sorenson. "I know several bars which still have bartenders and waitresses and customers. Some are cozy and quiet, just right for a little conversation.

"You were going to go home and tell hubby all about this crazy case, and the odd fellow who's at the center of it and doesn't tell you anything. Why not tell him with me there? Maybe he'll think of a question you haven't. Though I think that's not likely. Maybe you could double-team me to make me say something."

"What are you trying to get from me?" asked Radcliffe, peevishly.

"What makes you think I'm trying to get something from you?" replied Sorenson, innocently.

"Why do you always answer a question with a question?" asked Radcliffe.

"Do I really do that?" replied Sorenson.

"Hiya, honey, who's this?" asked a man coming out of the station. He was tall, almost six feet, and slender. He looked about forty years old, still with a spring in his step, even after a long day's work. His black hair was neither short nor long, carefully combed and parted. His suit was gray, with a pale shirt of a color hard to identify in the light of the parking lot.

"Hi, Paul," said Radcliffe, "this is tonight's mystery man, the guy I told you about earlier. He wants to take us both out for a drink, just to wrap up the night. His name, he said, is John Smith. Mahoney doesn't believe that and told him so. I don't believe that, either, but I'm too polite to say so to his face. He now says it is Jack Sorenson. Same initials, never a good sign."

"Nobody asks a cop out for a drink," Paul began.

"He doesn't say 'cop' ," said Radcliffe, "he says 'police' instead, every time."

"Really!?" said Paul, "how extraordinary. Nobody does that. I will rephrase that, then. Nobody asks a police personage out for a drink, not without some ulterior motive. What's your game?"

"I just like learning about people," said Sorenson. "I have interactions with the police more often than I would like, but it's all on a professional level. I think it would be nice to find out what a police inspector is like when off duty. Nothing personal, but do you have hobbies, where do you go for vacations, what team do you root for?

"Look, there's a nice, low-key bar a couple of blocks from here that stays open until two. We can walk there, have a quiet drink, and chat like ordinary people. And then you can go home, and I can go home, just like ordinary people. I know your wife wants to know more about me. It's easier to find out things over a drink. Or are you worried that the tail on me is going to snitch on you?"

"So, you're not slipping, after all," said Radcliffe. "Well, Paul, it's up to you. We've both had long days, and he really isn't going to tell either of us anything. But a free drink is sounding better and better all the time."

"OK, buddy," said Paul, "if you're buying, I'll have a drink. This *is* interesting, Phyllis. So much mystery over a non-crime. Much more intriguing than the thugs I usually deal with."

***

The bar was cozy, and quiet. The wallpaper looked new, although it didn't look very good. A piano near the bar suggested entertainment earlier in the evening, but the lid was down and the bench pushed under the piano. There was even a clear area that might be called a dance floor. There weren't many people in the place and the bartender looked bored. A waitress sat on a bar stool looking worn out, as if she had carried too many beers to too many tables tonight.

They had talked a little on the walk to the bar, mostly about what a pleasant night it was. As they neared the bar, Sorenson asked them what they wanted to drink. Inside, he let them pick a table and gave the barman their order – two whiskeys and a beer. The waitress shook herself awake, hoping for one last tip to make the late night worth while.

Once the waitress had given them their drinks and retired to her stool, Paul Radcliffe said, "Phyllis told me on the phone earlier today what you say you do. She said you claimed to stay on the fine edge of the law, but I have some doubts. Betting at the race track is legal in this state, and so is some off track betting, riverboat casinos, and the state lottery. Bookies don't fall into any of those categories, but you take bets to bookies.

"And arranging girls for men who want them is usually considered pimping, also on the wrong side of the law. Delivering monthly 'salaries' to rich men's mistresses isn't illegal, but one can argue the morality of it. You said you do other things, as well. Do you deliver bribes?"

"Ah, gee," said Sorenson, "and I was hoping for a nice, polite conversation about your flower garden. I do not knowingly deliver bribes. There. That's a straight answer for you, and absolutely true. I deliver money to people, and I am not always told why. The people who send me don't volunteer the information, and if they don't tell me, I never ask."

"What makes you think we have a flower garden?" asked Phyllis Radcliffe.

"Just a weak joke," said Sorenson, "though you might be the kind of people who would unwind from a stressful job by doing a little gardening. See, that's what I want to learn about you. Not just you two, but police officers in general. As Gilbert and Sullivan said,

> 'When the enterprising burglar's not a-burgling,
>   When the cut-throat isn't occupied in crime,
>   He loves to hear the little brook a-gurgling,
>   And listen to the merry village chime.'

So, what are you like when you're not sniffing out clues or turning thumbscrews?"

"We don't use thumbscrews any more," said Paul. "They make too much mess on the floor, and the janitors complained to their union. Do you think that knowing something about what cops do off duty will help you beat them on duty?"

"No. I know it won't," said Sorenson. "I told your wife that I know all about Detective Mahoney, not as an individual detective, but as a type. And he knows me. I know what I can get away with, with him. He knows what buttons aren't going to work with me. I haven't talked to you enough, but your wife is a new type to me. She's smart and sees further through a brick wall than most people. I need to understand her, and the others like her I'm likely to meet in the future.

"You complained that my visiting bookies and arranging girls was all illegal. Yes, it is, but only if I get caught doing it, and I won't be caught. I won't be caught, not because I have friends on the force, but because I know how the police handle bookies and prostitutes. All I have to do is avoid stepping wrong, and I won't be caught. You can't arrest me now because I've told you I sometimes place illegal bets, or hire prostitutes for guys. You have no evidence, just my say-so. And you know that if I was on trial, I'd tell the court I was just pulling your leg.

"I know how to skirt the line, but the line can shift. Where it is depends on how the police want to enforce the law. Tomorrow the chief of police might announce a new drive against prostitution in Berwyn. More policemen making more arrests. That would change how I do my job, maybe even what I am willing to do. And I need to know that before I get caught, so that I won't get caught. It's not just avoiding arrest. It's also knowing what things are going to be too dangerous for me to undertake. A pile of money doesn't do me any good if I'm in jail, or if I have to turn it over to some lawyer."

"How did you get started in this business?" asked Phyllis. "It doesn't seem like something you get into by answering an ad in the paper."

"Actually, that was how I got started," said Sorenson. "I was eighteen, fresh out of high school, and looking for work, any sort of work. My dad saw an ad for a waiter at a restaurant, and made me take it. This was about thirty years ago, and Detective Mahoney may remember Manny Devine's restaurant on Harlem. It was a restaurant downstairs, and a gambling hall upstairs. Manny dodged the health inspectors and such by saying the upstairs belonged to the Berwyn Geological Society. Who was going to check?

"I was a good waiter, and got promoted to the gambling hall. I made friends with the gamblers, and with Manny, and he and they would sometimes have me run small errands for them. A guy might send me to his house to ask his wife for more cash. Yeah, really.

"Manny used me to deliver messages for him. At that time Melissa's place was called Miriam's place. Miriam was Melissa's mother, and Melissa's grandmother had established the brothel back in the thirties.

"Manny wanted to get a few girls in the gambling hall for his customers, but Miriam wouldn't let her girls work anyplace but her brothel. She set the rules Melissa still follows, no rough guys, no abuse of the girls, just fun sex. Manny kept trying to get her to change her mind. He started out asking for five girls, which was crazy. He couldn't provide enough customers to keep five girls busy all night.

"I just delivered his messages, so I don't know this for sure, but I think he was trying to take over Miriam's business. Move the girls to his place, then drive Miriam out of business, maybe move his operation into her place. Miriam said no to his request for five girls. He suggested three, and she said no to that, as well. Then he made a big mistake. He asked for just one girl, but it had to be Melissa.

"Melissa never worked upstairs at Miriam's place, or now, either. Miriam valued her daughter too much to make her just another working girl. I delivered the message from Manny, and she turned red in the face. She asked me if I knew what he was asking for. I said I had typed it up as he dictated it. She asked me what I thought of it. I said I had tried to talk Manny out of it, but he wouldn't listen to me.

"She told me Manny's place would be shut down soon, and asked me if I wanted to work in her restaurant. I told her I would like that. I said that because I had seen the mayor going upstairs when I came in with Manny's message. I had just turned nineteen, but I knew who was going to win this fight.

She sent me back to Manny with a verbal reply. 'Get out of town while you can.'

"He laughed at her and I went home early. The next day the police were going upstairs at Manny's restaurant and he was shut down. He got sent to jail for gambling, and tax evasion. The gamblers went elsewhere to lose their money. And enough of them showed up at Miriam's that I was still serving them their meals, and sometimes running their errands.

"The errand business picked up and expanded into other things I won't tell you about. I was doing so well I quit the waiter job. Actually, I passed it on to Peterson, and told him about the lucrative side jobs he could get. He'd been working on a beer truck and was glad to get a better job, especially one with possibilities.

"And that is the story of my life. I always stayed on good terms with Miriam, and with Melissa when Miriam retired. Their place has often been a source of clients for me, and a fount of information about almost anything."

"I was right, Paul," said Phyllis, "he wasn't really going to tell us anything. But the drink was nice. Thank you for that. It looks like the bartender wants to go home, and the waitress is half asleep. Let's go home, dear, I'm as tired as she is. Am I going to have more trouble with you, Mr. Sorenson?"

"I certainly hope not," he replied.

***

The Radcliffes went back to the police parking lot, talking in low tones as they walked. Sorenson gave them only a casual glance to make sure of their destination, and a longer look to to find his shadow. He turned and went down the block, and around the corner to where he had parked that evening. He waited for the tail to turn the corner, and told him, "I'm going home now. I'll wait for you to get a car to follow me, if you want."

"Screw you!" said Markham. "Was I that obvious?"

"No," said Sorenson, "but I expected someone would tail me. And at this time of night, anyone on the street stands out. Do I wait for your car, or can I go home now?"

"Beat it," said the cop, disgustedly.

Sorenson drove off slowly and turned south, keeping to the speed limit so as not to lose the car that left the curb shortly after he did. He parked near his apartment building, locked his car, and went inside. The building was quiet, which was to be expected at "2:05" as his watch said.

Do I deliver bribes? How simple a view of bribery, he thought. *The man offering the bribe has to make the offer in person. The man receiving the bribe wants to see the man who is making the bribe. There's no role there for a go-between. Of course, once the bribe has been made and a relationship has been established, any further, continuing transfers of money should be called "payoffs". And payoffs can be handled by a go-between. Fortunately, Mr. Radcliffe had too limited, too legalistic a view of bribery.*

***

Paul and Phyllis Radcliffe talked about their unusual nightcap with Mr. Sorenson on their way home. It was only a ten minute drive, so they were still discussing his odd character and behavior when they got home.

Their house, like a great many of the houses in and near Chicago, was a bungalow style. In many neighborhoods they were practically identical, so many peas in a pod. They all had the same brick structure, using the same color bricks, the same shingles on the roof. Only the paint on the wood trim and the flowers in the front gardens made a difference in their appearance.

The houses in the Radcliffe's neighborhood were more varied than most, but there was still an impression of sameness. The Radcliffe's house was a little bigger than those of most of their neighbors, and a little nicer inside as well. The extra size showed up in the larger living room, with a comfortable sofa and chairs, and a large fireplace. The living room opened onto a dining room, with a kitchen behind it, and small side rooms off the dining room and kitchen.

Paul unlocked the front door, and turned on the light switch as they entered. They stopped cold, literally cold, shivering at what they saw.

The fireplace in their living room had a gaping hole in it, three feet across and tall. The debris covered the well-polished wood floor.

"My god, Paul," said Phyllis, shakily. "What… Someone's broken in, and… Have we been burgled?"

"Well, now we know why Sorenson wanted to keep us out so late," said Paul, pulling his gun from its holster. "Watch this door while I check out the rest of the house. And call for backup. It's going to be a long night."

He searched the house quickly, but thoroughly, and found only a smashed back door. By the time he returned to the living room, a patrol car was pulling up outside. Two uniformed policemen walked up to the door, and Phyllis let them in. Five minutes later another car pulled up and two detectives joined the crowd inside.

Paul and Phyllis gave statements about their evening. They didn't mention Sorenson because they knew where he was all evening. But they did decide to bring him in for some more questioning in the morning. Paul suggested Phyllis go to bed, since she had been up since six the previous morning. He stayed and replied "I don't know" to a lot of questions. It was almost surreal, watching policemen investigating a crime in his own home.

After the technicians had dusted and sprayed and photographed everything, he took a closer look at the back door. Smashed in, and not very carefully. The dent looked like a hefty sledge hammer made it. Which made sense, since a hefty sledge hammer would have been needed to destroy the fireplace.

Looking at the fireplace, he saw that the front was not just smashed, but that a hidden compartment had been exposed. A box about a foot and a half on each side sat on a shelf in the broken fireplace. It was empty, but must have contained something the burglars had been after. He looked for traces of an outline of something that might have sat in there, but saw nothing. There was dust and debris on the floor of the compartment that would have covered any other dust footprints.

The patrolmen had gone long ago, and the technicians were also leaving. The lead detective asked Paul, "Do you want me to leave someone here to keep watch over you, Inspector?"

"No," said Paul, "the burglars who did this won't come back. And any other self-respecting burglar has been in bed for hours, too. I think we'll be all right. I just want to get to bed myself."

"Well, we won't keep you up any longer sir," said the detective, "good night."

Chapter Four

Individual policemen may need to sleep, but police departments never do. At eight in the morning, Sorenson was awakened by a sturdy pounding on his door. Pulling on a robe and stumbling from his bedroom and across the living room, he opened the door to find Detective Mahoney and two uniformed cops.

"I have here a warrant," said Mahoney stiffly, "duly signed by Judge Felix McDermott authorizing a search of these premises. These two officers would like to join me in the exalted rank of detective, and they will find anything of interest in this apartment, including the collar button you lost two years ago. When they are through, you will accompany me back to the station house for another discussion. That is a request, not an order, but I think you will know how to respond."

"Of course I do, Detective Mahoney," said Sorenson, as cheerfully as he could. "Could they start with the bathroom – I'd like to take a shower? Where's Detective Inspector Radcliffe? I thought you'd both show up this morning."

"She has another matter to attend to," said Mahoney, "but it does involve you. That's why you're going to accompany us back to the office."

Unable to get anything more out of Mahoney, and the bathroom having already been searched, Sorenson stepped into the shower. By the time he had cleaned himself and shaved, his bedroom had been searched as well. He dressed in a plain tan suit and then went into the kitchen and fixed himself a quick cup of coffee. Checking the progress of the search, he decided he had time to make an omelet and a couple of slices of toast for a proper breakfast.

Meanwhile the two policemen continued combing through the apartment. It was a spacious one bedroom apartment on the second floor of a small apartment building. The bedroom was big enough for a queen sized bed, dresser, and nightstand. The living room was much larger, almost too large for a man who lived alone. A nicely patterned couch and two matching chairs faced opposite sides of a coffee table.

One wall held a large bookcase, most of whose shelves were full of books. Another wall was occupied by a large, but not immense, television. Beneath that was a small cabinet containing the usual components of a home entertainment center. The only clock in the apartment was part of the cable box. A small writing desk and chair faced a window overlooking the street.

The policemen were thorough, but neat, and left everything as they had found it. Even the books were carefully shaken out and placed back on the shelves. He was impressed. It took them just over two hours to open every drawer, poke into every crevice in his couch, and check the contents of his pantry. It helped that he kept very little of importance here.

"OK, let's go, Sorenson," said Mahoney. "Time for some more fun and games at the police station. Only this time, you're going to have a shorter leash."

"Why is that, Detective?" asked Sorenson.

"You'll find out when we get downtown," said Mahoney, pushing him out the door.

***

Sorenson was brought into the same interrogation room he had occupied the night before. Detective Inspector Radcliffe was waiting inside. This time Mahoney read him his Miranda rights. Sorenson's eyebrows went up.

"Am I under arrest, then?" he asked.

"Not yet," said Mahoney, "I'm just saving time. Yesterday you were an unusual non-witness to something bizarre. Today you are considered a 'person of interest', as we say."

"What happened at my house last night, and why?" asked Radcliffe, bluntly.

"I have no idea," answered Sorenson, casually. "I don't even know where you live. Or if you live in a house or an apartment. After we parted last night, I went home. You can check with the tail you put on me. I even drove slowly so he wouldn't lose me."

"Were you deliberately keeping my husband and me up till all hours for some nefarious reason?"

"Nefarious? Hmmm. I was just trying to be sociable, and buy you a drink," said Sorenson. "Is drinking now nefarious?"

"You keep dodging my questions, and I don't like that," said Radcliffe angrily. "You are going to give me some straight answers or you are going to be locked up for conspiracy in a burglary. Now, why was my house burgled and vandalized last night?"

"This is the first I've heard of any burglary or vandalism," said Sorenson, "at your house or any other place. I don't know anything about it. I didn't know it happened until you just told me. I didn't know it was going to happen. I like staying up late, and I like having company when I do. As I told you last night, I also like to learn how people act and think off duty."

"The search of your apartment this morning turned up a bank receipt," said Radcliffe. "You deposited $3,000 yesterday. That's considerably more than you had on you yesterday afternoon. Where did it come from? Who gave it to you? Why did they give it to you?"

"Between our meeting at the empty bar, and my showing up here last evening," said Sorenson, "I picked up another job. I sometimes go a week or two without fresh work, and then two or three jobs fall out of the sky all at once. That's all. I don't really know why they would pay me so much, but I don't ask a lot of questions about my jobs.

"The people who hire me assume I know how to do what they want done. I can legitimately ask for an address or someone's name. Asking the 'why' question about a job is asking to go on unemployment. Someone else will get this job, and no one else will ever give me another job. I'm sometimes anonymous. My clients are often anonymous. The jobs are almost always anonymous."

"That's a nice little speech," said Radcliffe, "but it doesn't actually answer my questions, does it? I know so much about *how* you do your job, and so very little about what you really do. Lock him up, Mahoney. We'll see if a little time by himself in a cell will loosen his tongue."

Mahoney asked Sorenson to stand up, and then handcuffed him.

"I don't really have to do this," he said, "it just makes me feel good."

***

Mahoney took Sorenson down a different corridor, down a flight of stairs, and through a door into a room with a chest high counter marred by ink stains. While Mahoney filled out the paperwork to book Sorenson for conspiracy in a burglary, a uniformed policeman unlocked the cuffs. He then put an ink pad and a printed form with one inch square boxes on the counter and instructed Sorenson to give them a set of nice, neat fingerprints. Sorenson was just using a rag to wipe the ink off of his fingers when two other policemen came in.

"He was dead as dead can be," said the first cop. "Shot at close range in the back of the head. Looks like a gangland killing, but they usually do a double-tap."

"Gangland? I doubt it." said his partner. "Name's George Peterson. I used to work with the major crimes guys, and I never heard of anyone by that name. No matter, all we have to do is drop our little report off here and let somebody else work it out."

Sorenson didn't blink when he heard Peterson's name, but he was quiet all the way to the cell. He sat down and started to think. *I called Peterson "Pete," everybody did, as a nickname. Most people only knew him that way. But I know Peterson's first name was George. Common enough name, actually, but I don't like coincidences. Especially ones involving jobs I'm doing.*

If this dead guy is my George Peterson, I could tell Inspector Radcliffe that Peterson had paid me, and hadn't told me why. I could even mention I was supposed to keep her and her husband out until at least two in the morning. Should I do that? The job was a secret, something in trust. But in trust to Peterson, who is now dead, and beyond caring about broken trusts. In other circumstances, I might owe something to the man who had paid Peterson. But if that man is responsible for killing Pete, I don't owe him anything. Not that I know who he is, anyway.

Would Inspector Radcliffe even be satisfied with the little I can tell her. "I got fifteen grand to keep you away from home until the middle of the night. That's all I know, honest." Yeah, she'll believe that. Sure she will. A ten year old wouldn't accept that as all I know. And yet it is.

Pity about Peterson, he was a good man. And a careful man, someone who didn't normally let people get behind him with a gun. And if someone killed Peterson because he was the go-between between the burglars and me, would Peterson be the only link they would eliminate? Or would he be only the first one, because he knew who paid him? Would they come for the cat's paw, too?

If I'm vulnerable, telling the police what little I know might be useful. Tying Peterson's death to the burglary might help the police find his murderer. It might also offer me a little protection, if the police think I'd be more use to them alive than dead. Talking to the police might get me out of this cell, but did I really want to be walking the streets right now? If someone is looking to kill me, too, this might be the safest place to be.

***

"On your feet, fella," said the guard, "they want you back upstairs again. Ain't you lucky."

It was the same interrogation room. Sorenson wondered if there others, or if this was the only one the station had. The room was more crowded now, too. Detective Mahoney and Detective Inspector Radcliffe were now joined by Detective Inspector (Mr.) Radcliffe and a stenographer. An extra chair had been brought in for the stenographer.

"Ah, the mysterious Mr. Sorenson, how are you this morning?" asked Paul Radcliffe. "I hear they had you up before breakfast this morning. How sad. I didn't ask you up from your cozy cell just to ask you about how many meals you've missed today, however. I just found a picture of you, and you'll never guess where I found it."

"Is it still morning?" asked Sorenson. "They took my watch when they booked me. I hope I don't have to add lunch to the list of missed meals. A picture, you say. I didn't know there were any pictures of me in circulation. Other than the ones you take downstairs."

"This **is** you, isn't it?" asked Paul Radcliffe, showing him a picture of two men in a bar. "Who's the other man?"

"Ah, I like policemen who only ask questions they know the answers to," replied Sorenson. "That's a friend of mine named George Peterson, though everybody called him 'Pete'."

"And how did you know we already knew the answer?" asked Phyllis Radcliffe.

"The booking office is also apparently the social center of this police station," replied Sorenson. "I overheard two policemen talking about a dead man they had to file a report on. His name was George Peterson. I don't believe in coincidences."

"Ah, we have something in common," said Paul Radcliffe, "policemen don't believe in coincidences, either. So, if you don't think anyone has a picture of you, why did he have one?"

"That was taken about three years ago," said Sorenson. "We were celebrating winning a big bet. I forget what the teams were, but we picked the underdog, bet big, and made a nice pile of cash. I don't remember who took the picture, must have been one of his other friends. I forgot he had it. He carried it around as a good luck charm – I had suggested the bet, and he thought I was going to keep bringing him good luck. I guess there's a time limit on good luck charms. What happened to him?"

"He was found this morning in his apartment, shot in the back of his head," said Paul Radcliffe. "The door was ajar and another tenant, walking past, saw him and told the building super. He checked it out and called us. Peterson had been dead for several hours when the ME got there. He estimates time of death at about midnight or one. Lucky for you. You've got two cops to be your alibi."

"So now we come back to my persistent question," said Phyllis Radcliffe. "Why were you keeping us out all night? What did Peterson have to do with that? Is that what the $3,000 was for? Why was he killed?"

"Technically, that last question is your husband's," said Sorenson, "but I'll answer it for you anyway. I honestly do not know. Neither of us knowingly did anything with any risk of death. And, even so, he was a very careful man. He used to fantasize being a secret agent, with secret meetings and payoffs, just like the movies. But he avoided the danger part of that image.

"I will tell you everything I do know, now that Peterson is dead. I was trying to protect him earlier because he was my friend, but now I don't have to.

"He had asked to meet me at that bar yesterday at four o'clock. He was a very punctual man, so if he said four o'clock, he would be there no later than four, and usually a bit early. But he wasn't there, and there was no sign of him having been there. We aren't in the thug end of the seamy side of the city, but he could take care of himself. If someone had tried to kidnap him, there would be signs of a serious struggle.

"After I left the bar, I went looking for him. I didn't know where he was because he wasn't where he had said he'd be. So I went to the park near his apartment. Being a spy nut, he used a bench there as a place to leave messages. I was going to check for a message, but I found him instead.

"He told me about the fake kidnapping, everything. He said he used a mask, but he didn't say what the mask was. That's why Abraham Lincoln fooled me. He said the whole point of the kidnapping was so that I could meet you, Mrs. Radcliffe. He told me to go down to the station about seven in the evening and say I had received a phone call about the kidnapping. I was to string you along as long as I could, preferably without mentioning him.

"I was supposed to keep you away from your house until at least two, any way I could. The money was my fee, and it was actually fifteen grand. I deposited it before coming here last night, and put some into my safe deposit box. I have no idea why I was paid so much. It's way more than I should have been paid for playing games with the police. I have no idea who put up the money. Peterson didn't tell me, and I knew he wouldn't if I had asked. Like I said earlier, 'why' is not a question my clients like to hear."

"So, when we get this typed up," asked Mahoney, "will you be nice for once, and sign this confession?"

"What confession?" asked Sorenson. "I was supposed to meet a man at a bar, and he didn't show up. No crime there. I knew nothing about the kidnapping until later. You can't connect me with that. I helped you recover the victims of the fake kidnapping. I should get a pat on the back for that, at least."

"If you had told us Peterson's role in the kidnapping," said Mahoney, "we would have picked him up and he'd still be alive."

"Yeah, that occurred to me, too," said Sorenson, "but that's hindsight. At the time, I was trying to provide cover for him, not get him arrested for a serious crime. I didn't know he was going to be killed, and neither did he.

"I did keep two hard working police officers from their beauty sleep for quite a while last night. I'm not sure if that's a crime or not. I did do this knowing that someone unknown to me wanted it done. And that suggests that that unknown someone had some also unknown ulterior motive for wanting to keep you out all night. But I do not know this person, or his motive, or even, now that I think of it, just what he did to your house."

"The back door was broken in," said Paul Radcliffe, "and a very large hole was made in our fireplace. And that's all that was done. This hole revealed a large cavity where we believe something had once been hidden. I don't suppose you know what that might have been, either."

"How very curious," said Sorenson, thoughtfully. "You're the one slipping now, Mrs. Radcliffe. You have both missed the most important clue. And the most puzzling one. I can't figure it out, but I see it plainly."

"Oh, for god's sake, stop being so mysterious," shouted Phyllis Radcliffe. "We haven't told you anything about the crime scene or what clues we've found. How could you know we've missed one?"

"You normally work until eight o'clock, your husband works until around one. With the extra time you spent going out to rescue the kidnap victims, talking to them, and then talking to me, you weren't ready to go home until after midnight. From after dark, say eight o'clock this time of year, to midnight is plenty of time to break into someone's house and smash his fireplace.

"So, why should I keep you out later? My part in the earlier half of the evening was a little suspicious, but not enough to get hauled in for more questioning. I'm here now only because I kept you out longer than any reasonably good burglar needed to do his job. Why? I confess, I don't know. But that is the clue you both missed."

"Ouch," said Phyllis Radcliffe, "a clue as big as that and I missed it. I'll blame it on lack of sleep last night."

"You're a clever man, Mr. Sorenson," said Paul Radcliffe. "You're right, we should have both seen that clue, and so should you, Mahoney. You don't even have the excuse of a long night. You say you don't know why, but you're clever. Would you venture a guess?"

"No, not even a wild ass guess," said Sorenson. "But I'll tell you how I would think, will think, about this. The time is important in some way. Why couldn't they break in earlier? They knew where the thing was they were looking for, because they found it without having to damage anything but your fireplace. So they didn't need the time to search the place.

"And if Peterson was killed between midnight and one, was that before or after the break-in? If after, why keep you out until two? If before the break-in, then, again, why break-in so late? Peterson read spy novels. I read true crime stories. I don't plan crimes, but I like reading about people who do. If this was a story, I wouldn't have had any role but the one I played yesterday afternoon.

"Once the police get involved, anyone can make an anonymous call to the station and get you out for most of the evening. I'm not needed to do that. I'm also not needed to keep you out late, because the burglary can be done long before midnight. And Peterson doesn't need to tell me anything, or pay me anything. And he shouldn't be killed, because no one is going to connect him with any of this, so no one will question him about his paymaster."

"If Peterson did the kidnapping," said Phyllis Radcliffe, "he must be the one who faked the surveillance tapes. That took time and breaking into the bar's office to get an old tape. He was more than just a messenger on this job. They may have been afraid he'd figure out what they were doing, or hear about what was taken, and try to make a buck off of it."

"I never knew Peterson to try to blackmail someone," said Sorenson. "The kind of people we work for, that's not always a good idea, and he knew that. I said, he was careful. And he didn't ask any more questions than I do. He probably had no more idea about what was going on when he died,, than we do now. And if I got $15,000, he must have gotten more, for doing the kidnapping and setting me up. Have you found his cut?"

"Not yet," said Mahoney, "but we haven't had much time to look for his bank yet. There was nothing in his apartment, but the killer may have taken the money."

"Anything else you can tell us, Mr. Sorenson?" asked Paul Radcliffe. "Anything Peterson might have said about what you were to do? Any suggestion of who might be behind the job?"

"No, nothing," said Sorenson. "But you might want to check his dead drop. I told you he liked to fantasize about being a spy. There's a bench in the park by his place, and there's a small hole in the right end of the bench. He used to leave messages for people there. Sometimes someone else would leave him a message. You might want to take a look and see if there's anything there. Very few people knew about this, and I doubt if his killer did."

"Did you hang out with Peterson? Ever been to his apartment?" asked Mahoney.

"We were friends," said Sorenson, "fairly close friends for the kind of work we do. We went to high school together. But we didn't go visiting each other at home. That's what bars are for, and they're not going to be bugged. You can get a booth away from other people and talk privately. We talked sometimes about jobs we had for one another. We talked sometimes about the people who gave us these jobs. And, no, I have no idea who gave Pete this job. If I did, I'd give him up to you in a flash."

"If you didn't ask questions, how did you know enough about these guys to talk about them?" asked Mahoney.

"You can learn a lot without asking questions," said Sorenson. "We're smart men, not book smart, but street smart. We can read between the lines, sometimes even if there are no lines. We would pay attention to the people a man has working for him. Maybe we've seen them someplace else. We would often check up the man's address, home or business, to find out who he really was. That's how you stay out of drug deals. You turn down that man's jobs."

"Could you turn down a job?" asked Phyllis Radcliffe. "Drug dealers are tough guys who don't like being told no."

"True," said Sorenson, "but they can't tell if you're lying when you say you're busy with somebody else's job that night. Pete and I were well known, and we made sure everybody knew we didn't do certain kinds of jobs. If the dealer knows in advance you're not going to take his job, he won't offer it to you."

"You told me you didn't do truly illegal jobs," said Phyllis Radcliffe, "what about Peterson? Would he have been knowingly involved in a really serious crime?"

"Well, he told me he did the kidnapping," said Sorenson, "which is a pretty serious crime. But he didn't think anyone was going to connect him to the crime, and I think he figured the crime would fall off everyone's radar before too long. He may have known about the burglary, or guessed it. If so, he didn't tell me.

"He sometimes cut closer to the edge of the law than I normally do, but he usually tried to stay on the safe side. This time he tried to make it a safe kidnapping; even the shotgun was unloaded. He kept the victims prisoners for as short a time as possible. He always thought that if no one knew he was involved in something, then he was safe. I doubt he would have taken the job, though, if he knew there might be violence. Especially against himself."

"Do you know any of the people he did jobs for?" asked Paul Radcliffe.

"A few of them," said Sorenson, "we both handled some of the same guys making dubious payouts to people. If one of us was busy that day, the other would take the job. But these are small-time players, not guys capable of organizing something like this. The bigger fish were more particular about whom they dealt with. One man, and one man only. And often their own men.

"Still, I mentioned we talked about our bosses from time to time. I can't think of any of them who would or could pull this off. But, while we shared secrets, we did not share all of our secrets. I held out on him about some people, and he probably held out on me."

"So you're not going to help us?" said Mahoney, bitterly.

"I am helping you as much as I can," said Sorenson. "I just don't know very much about what happened or why. I've put you on to the timetable problem. That's important – why did the actual break-in have to be so late at night? You've got a whole police department here at your disposal. Have some of your bloodhounds sniff out these suggestions.

Make up more yourself. Detective Mahoney's got the experience to handle this. Turn him loose on it."

"You trying to make nice with me?" asked Mahoney.

"You know me, Detective Mahoney," said Sorenson, "and I know you. You know me as just a high-paid fixer, and I know you as a police officer who despises any sort of fixer, even the high-paid ones. But I also know that you do know your stuff. I can almost smell competence, and you reek of it. I don't like having you chasing after me, it's bad for my business. I'd rather have you chase someone else."

"Okay, Mahoney," said Paul Radcliffe with a grin, "Mr. Sorenson has given you his personal endorsement. Please return the favor and let him go. You know the routine, I'm sure, Sorenson -- don't leave town. Keep in touch. Let us know anything else that happens to you, or that occurs to you. Oh, and I'm sorry that we did make you miss lunch, too."

Nobody offered to shake his hand or say good-bye, so Sorenson just followed Mahoney back to the booking office downstairs. He signed the paperwork and took back his watch, wallet, phone, and other pocket items. Mahoney had gone as soon as he signed his paperwork, and Sorenson had to ask the clerk for the shortest way out of the station house.

Chapter Five

Mahoney went back to his desk after releasing Sorenson on Wednesday afternoon. It was almost four, a whole day since he first met Sorenson, and only more mysteries to show for it. *Too many mysteries, too few clues,* he thought. *I'm a detective, but how can I detect without clues. A kidnapping, a burglary, a murder. What next? All connected somehow, but how? One man who knows about some parts of the mystery, but is he telling us all he knows?*

"Get your hat, Sam," Phyllis Radcliffe told Mahoney, "I'm going to do something cops never get to do. I'm going to work from home."

"Think there's anything to see there," said Mahoney. "The forensics boys did a good job last night while you and Paul slept."

"I know," said Phyllis, "good, and quiet, too. Paul said he stayed up until they left, but they were quick. But they were looking for fingerprints and DNA and hairs. There are no fingerprints because these guys are professionals. And the rest only helps convict them if we arrest them and have some samples to compare the hairs to.

"No, I want to look for the non-forensic clues. That's why I need you along. Two pairs of eyes might see things that one pair will miss. I was too tired last night, and too outraged and scared to look properly. Let's take the time to look everything over carefully, and think about every broken brick."

Fifteen minutes later they were standing in the doorway to Phyllis' house, looking at the debris still strewn across the floor. There were bricks everywhere, and everything was covered with a heavy layer of broken mortar and dust. She had given orders last night for the investigators to leave the mess as it was. They had, of course, trampled all over it in their search for trace evidence, but the general pattern was intact.

A ragged hole, three feet square, stared blankly at them like an empty eye socket. The bottom of the hole was just above the mantle piece. The burglars had brought a kitchen chair into the living room and placed it in front of the fireplace. It was just the right height for the man with the sledge to stand on and reach the spot he wanted to smash. Both mantle and chair were covered in mortar, dust, and bits of brick.

The fireplace was of an unusual design, the brickwork wider than needed for the hearth and chimney, and tall, reaching to the ceiling. The mantle was fastened to the brickwork about a foot above the hearth opening. The brickwork was broken only on the right side of the fireplace, and no other part showed any sign of damage.

Inside the hole was an open-sided box, about a foot and a half square and two feet tall. Its bottom was covered in dust, much of it from the destruction of the brickwork, but some accumulated from age. There was a small mark on one side as if some metal object had been used to force a cover off the box, but no sign of the cover and there were no hinges.

Radcliffe and Mahoney stood side by side peering into the gaping hole. Phyllis took a small measuring tape from her pocket and measured the hole, the box, the distance of the box from the sides of the hole, the depth of the hole, the distance of the box from the chimney. Mahoney dutifully noted down all the measurements in his notebook, and sighed when she had finished.

"The only measurements you needed to take were the size of the box," he said, "because the thing taken had to fit inside it. And the thing taken could have been much smaller than the box."

"I know, but I didn't want to overlook anything," said Phyllis. "Once we repair the damage, we won't be able to re-examine this. This is all that's damaged, the only thing in the whole house except the back door, where they came in. They knew something was hidden here, and must have known exactly where it was hidden.   Something not too big, but something obviously valuable. What? What?"

"And when was it put in there?" asked Mahoney. "Someone took the time to make a hideaway for this thing, planning to come back for it. This has been here since before you bought the house. This would have taken time to do. If someone had done this when you and Paul were on vacation, you would have noticed the change in the brickwork. And look at the dust here, in this box. Here's the dust from the bricks, in front. And here's a different type of dust in the back, grayer, finer, more uniform. And it looks like someone has smudged that dust."

"They may have made the box in advance of needing it," said Phyllis, "and left it exposed. How fussy are criminals about housekeeping? Would they have cared about the dust?"

"Of course not," said Mahoney, "and the dust may have been disturbed when the thing was removed. It could have been taken out of here years ago, and put in years before that."

"Was it?" asked Phyllis. "Suppose some crooks hide something valuable here, planning to come back later. They replace the bricks and make it all look nice. At any later time, including the next day, any of them could have come back to take it for himself."

"What if only one guy did the whole thing?" asked Mahoney. "No, wait, that can't be it. He wouldn't need to break everything up because he would have known he had already taken it. And no one else would have known it was there."

"That means the dust is a red herring," said Phyllis. "The thing was here all this time, sitting on a bed of dust. Look, only the crooks who put the thing in here would come back for it. They knew exactly where to find it. They weren't working off of someone else's description of where to look. So the same bunch hid it and retrieved it."

"That makes sense," said Mahoney, "but one of the gang could still have taken it earlier and disappeared. Or disposed of it for the cash value, and stayed in the gang, pretending not to be rich. He acts as surprised as the others when the fireplace is opened up and it's empty."

"This was worth a lot of money," said Phyllis. "Sorenson admits getting $15,000 for his small part, and figures Peterson got even more for his larger role. This has got to be worth a great deal, more than a hundred grand anyway."

"They may not have paid Peterson anything but a bullet in the head," said Mahoney. "But you're probably right about the value. It wouldn't have been worth killing someone for a small prize."

"Yes, and if it was so valuable," said Phyllis, "would any crook taking it for himself sit quietly on it for several years? Wouldn't he find some excuse to leave the gang a long time ago, and enjoy his new wealth? Would his friends even know how well he was doing after he left?"

"Probably not," said Mahoney. "He could leave and move somewhere else and never contact them again. Most crooks like to stay in one place – they know their friends, their enemies, the police, it makes life easier for them. But they sometimes leave town, they sometimes have to leave town. And none of their friends is going to send a postcard asking how they're doing.

"But that still leaves us with the two possibilities. One of the gang snatched the thing right after they hid it here, as shown by the dust. Or it was still here until last night, and the dust means nothing. I can see it either way. In fact, even though I suggested it, I think the idea the thing was taken a long time ago is hooey, and that it was here yesterday.

"Look, the gang puts a big hole in this fireplace, puts a box in the hole, and puts a thing of value in the box. Then they patch the hole. If the house belongs to someone not in the gang, he's going to notice the repaired brickwork. And he's going to be in the way of someone trying to get the thing shortly after. And he's going to notice the bricks have been replaced twice. So the work was done once."

"Right, but if a gang member owns the house," said Phyllis, "he can open the hole any time he wants, and he won't complain about his own re-bricking work. And would any of the other gang members trust him to guard the loot?"

"Unless he was the boss," said Mahoney. "No one is going to challenge the boss' right to guard the loot. Would he cheat the rest of the gang? I've known some bosses who would, but most bosses don't want to have to put a new gang together every time they do a job."

"We are getting nowhere with this," said Phyllis, dejectedly. "And it's getting late. I'll drive you back to the station so you can get your car and go home. Tomorrow, take a look through our database for crooks who have brick-laying experience. Maybe they had a pro in the gang. The brickwork looked pretty good to me, before they smashed it.

"I'm going to visit my realtor, and see if she can give me a list of the owners of this house before we bought it. We got it from a bank in a foreclosure sale, but I'd like to know who they foreclosed on. And then I can come back here and clean up this mess. Ugh."

***

It was a quarter past six and Diane Fielding was still in her office, waiting for a possible evening client. Someone coming in after work to talk about buying or selling a house. She was sitting in front of her computer screen, looking over some new real estate listings from her rivals, when Phyllis arrived. She got up from her desk and welcomed her visitor.

"Phyllis Radcliffe, isn't it?" she asked. "How are you today? Looking to move to a new home already? Considering what prices are like today, and what a bargain you got on that house, you could do very well by selling now."

"No, we're not selling just yet," said Phyllis. "We like the house, and aren't looking to raise our mortgage payments. I'm actually here on my business."

"Your business?" asked Diane, "oh, that's right, you're with the police department. Surely there wasn't anything illegal about the sale, was there?"

"No," said Phyllis, "but the house was burgled last night, and some damage was done to the fireplace. It's odd to have to investigate my own house, but convenient in a way. I think something had been hidden in the fireplace by a former owner, and removed by the burglars last night. So I thought you might be able to give me a list of the owners over the last ten or fifteen years."

"Something hidden in the fireplace!?" said Diane in amazement, "how odd. But, yes, I can check our records for previous sales. I will have to go into the county realty records database to check that far back, especially since we may have only handled that property for your purchase. Please, sit down while I start the search. It shouldn't take too long. Would you like a cup of coffee while you wait?"

"Yes, thank you, I'll help myself," said Phyllis, going over to a coffee maker on a small side table. "Everybody jokes about cops going to coffee shops all the time, but without coffee, crime would run rampant throughout the country. When there aren't enough hours in a day, there's always coffee. I suppose it's the same for every busy profession.

"How far back can you check the records on house sales? And can you check sales through other realtors? Do you share that sort of information?"

"We have a feature here, as a realty office," said Diane, "that other people, buyers and sellers, don't have access to. If you searched for your house yourself, you might find the last couple of sale prices, but you wouldn't find any names. I can find the names, as well. And…. here we are. A longer list than I would have expected, seven names over the last fifteen years, including you. I'll print it out for you."

"Just the names and years, if you can do that," said Phyllis. "I don't really need any more than that."

"OK," said Diane. "Here, back in 2003 it was sold by the Johnsons, who were the original owners, according to this. They sold to, well, just look at the list."

`Year	Seller	Buyer
2003	Fred Johnson	Thomas Morgan
2004	Thomas Morgan	Ralph Reisler
2006	Ralph Reisler	Maxwell Donaldson
2009	Maxwell Donaldson	Arthur Falkenberg
2012	Arthur Falkenberg	Dennis Hoover
2014	Dennis Hoover	Pablo Rodriguez
2016	Bank foreclosure`	Paul and Phyllis Radcliffe

"That's wonderful, Diane," said Phyllis. "This should be just what I need. Thank you so much for your assistance. And, if we do ever decide to sell, we'll come to you."

***

Phyllis Radcliffe stopped at a diner for a quick supper. There was food in the refrigerator at home, and a home cooked meal would have been very nice. But there was also a big mess on the floor of her living room, and seeing that would have ruined her appetite. And dinner at home would have taken time and energy to cook. The diner's stew was canned, but tolerable, with a few chunks of extra meat thrown in so they could call it "home made" without too much embarrassment.

When she got home at last, she was at least fed, a little less tired for the chance to sit down at the diner, and resigned to the work ahead of her. Paul should be helping, but he was still on duty. She had told him earlier that she had planned to come back and re-examine the scene, and would he please not clean it up. And she couldn't put it off until he came home after midnight.

First things first, a little music to make the work less intolerable. WDCB played good jazz all the time, and good jazz always helped any work. Phyllis turned on the stereo and lowered the volume – not too loud, just enough to fend off the frustration of the job.

She began by spreading some newspapers on the sofa, in order to keep it clean. Well, not any dirtier, there was already plenty of dust and brick fragments on it. The she started picking up the whole bricks and stacking them on the paper. They would have to be moved again, later, but it would be more of an effort to pick them up off the floor a second time.

The larger pieces of broken brick joined the whole bricks on the sofa. There were still a large number of small fragments scattered over the floor, and an awful lot of dust. The mortar seemed to have been ground into smithereens by the forensics technicians. Armed with broom and dustpan, she swept up most of the remaining debris. As she finished sweeping, she realized that some of the debris had gone under the sofa.

She looked at the sofa, loaded with bricks, and decided that she would clean under there after they had gotten rid of the bricks. Then she got out the vacuum to pick up the finest dust particles. It had taken her two hours to get the room clean, but the job was done.

Phyllis went to the kitchen and took a squat glass from a cupboard. She put a couple of ice cubes from the freezer into it and went to the liquor cabinet to get the bottle of Bushmills. She poured some whiskey into the glass, a finger's worth, no, a finger and a half. It had been a long day. She brought the glass back to the living room, and her favorite chair. She set the glass on a small table by the chair and was just about to sit down when she spotted the mantle piece.

Focusing on the floor, she had forgotten to clean the mantle piece. Sighing, she got a brush and the dustpan and started clearing the small fragments littering the shelf. As she brushed the bits into the dustpan, she noticed a small scrap of paper falling to the floor. She picked it up and looked at it. It was slightly crusted with mortar, which she brushed off. One side was blank, the other had "Starp1102109" scrawled on it. She set it next to her drink and finished cleaning the mantle.

Settled comfortably in her chair, with a long sip of the whiskey inside her, and Ellington in the background, she picked up the scrap of paper. *What could it mean, and where did it come from? The handwriting isn't mine, or Paul's, and I know there was nothing on the mantle except the clock that's now broken. Did the burglars leave it behind by accident? Why would they? "Starp" was nothing like "Radcliffe", and the number bore no relation to their address, or their phone numbers.*

Did it fall out of the hole in the fireplace, somehow? Perhaps, but what was it doing there in the first place? Or maybe one of the burglars did drop it carelessly. Maybe it was his contact, or was 110-2109 a real phone number? Would a burglar still need the name and number of his partner when they were busy burgling? If he had it with him, wouldn't it be stuck in his pocket? Or was it the name and number of the big boss, so they could call him when the job was done? That made some sense.

Too many questions. Not enough sleep the night before. Too much work today, and tonight. Too little whiskey left in the glass. Finish it off and go to bed. Questions could wait for the morning.

Chapter Six

It was a nice sunny afternoon out when Sorenson left the police station after his interrogation. There was a burger joint down the street from the police station. He turned the other way and walked a couple of blocks to another restaurant. The first place was probably too popular with the police, and he really didn't want to spend too much more time with them today. His pork chop sandwich was dry, but the coffee was worth having a second cup.

He had shut his mind down after leaving the police station. He needed to give his subconscious time to work on the problem. Worrying too hard wasn't going to help any, and might drive away a good idea. And he needed a good idea.

Refreshed by his late lunch, he walked down the sidewalk, stopping every so often to look in shop windows and check discreetly for someone tailing him. He didn't see anyone, but he kept looking. The police tails were often good, but predictable. Criminals might be tailing him, too, to finish him the way they had Peterson. And a criminal tail would usually be more obvious from lack of practice, but much less predictable.

Three blocks from the restaurant, he found a bus just pulling up to a stop, and got on. No one else got on with him, or ran up too late. He took the bus for several blocks, then transferred to another that brought him to Peterson's front door. He got off and went into the park and sat on Peterson's bench. He felt for the hole at the end of it, and pulled out a single slip of paper. It had the name "Falkenberg" written on it.

He took the next bus back the way he had come, and stayed on it until it reached the train station. Another bus took him north to a residential neighborhood of bungalows and two-flats. An old brownstone stood on one corner, clean but battered by age. He went inside and up the stairs to the third floor. Using a key from the bunch on his key ring, he opened the door. Jack Sorenson disappeared, and Jeremy Snyder went into his apartment.

It had been three weeks since he was here last, and there was a thin layer of dust on the furniture. There actually wasn't very much furniture to get dusty. This apartment was smaller than the other with little to show anyone lived here. The bedroom was smaller, but not the bed, and there was no nightstand. The living room had two comfortable chairs, mismatched, and a small table between them. Another small writing desk and chair rounded off the contents of the apartment.

He went into the kitchen and checked the refrigerator – one six-pack of porter. *Good enough for a few days, but I'll have to get some more. Maybe some food, too. Restaurants might be dangerous for a while. Time to turn the mind back on and think this through.*

Peterson probably didn't know who he was really working for. He might have been willing to help burglars have access to a house, but most burglars weren't killers. He wouldn't have taken a job that involved any personal danger. So someone who posed as a burglar but who was really something more, or who was working for someone else. Still no ideas there.

And who is Falkenberg? Was he Pete's contact? If he was, was it a real name? Was he the man behind the plot? If he was, how did Pete learn his name? Surely the crook didn't let his own go-betweens use his name so casually. Could he be the man who hid something at the Radcliffes' house? Again, if he was, how did Pete come to know his name? Too many questions.

The police let me go, and without putting a tail on me. That probably means they believe my story, or enough of it to not need me any more for now. That's good, but a police tail might help keep me safe on the streets. There was no other tail, either. Which means the criminals don't care about me, or didn't want to try tailing me from the station house. They wouldn't have known I was being released this afternoon, so maybe they weren't ready to tail me yet. If so, they'll stake out my other apartment. This one is safe, and I'll probably be safe in the neighborhood, too.

So, get some groceries, at least enough for breakfast and lunch for a few days, and some more beer. There are two good restaurants within two blocks, and a bus can take me to other safe neighborhoods for other restaurants. My car is at the other apartment, most likely under observation. Best to leave it there.

He left the apartment, went downstairs, and checked the street. There was no one standing around within sight, so he went out and down to the local grocery store. It was a small mom-and-pop store, a rare survivor of an earlier day. A supermarket would be cheaper, but less convenient. This was in his neighborhood here. The Dvoraks had inherited the store from their parents and grandparents. They treated their customers well, offering what bargains they could, shifting their ethnic stock from Czech to Mexican as the years passed.

And the people in the neighborhood were glad to have a friendly store just down the street. The necessities of breakfast and lunch were easily obtained and bagged. The liquor store up the street sold him another six-pack of porter. He was set for a while.

But he would still have to go out to see and hear what was going on in his world. And that meant exposing himself to attack, or being followed back here. There was risk in going out but he needed the information that might be floating around out there. People who might talk to him would have heard already about Peterson, and they might have a tiny clue to give him. A face seen, a word overheard, anything might help. A lot of little bits could combine into a really big clue.

He would need some money to help loosen tongues. He checked his watch – it was too late to go to his bank for some of that $15,000 – even Friendly Banks had to close sometime. And the bank might be watched. He went to the dresser in the bedroom and pulled out the middle drawer. Turning it over, he removed the tape holding an envelope on the bottom of the drawer. The $2,000 in the envelope would have to do for now. If it wasn't enough, he had more problems than he thought he did.

The bookcase in the living room held an odd assortment of books and a several DVD cases. He read the books when he was holed up here, but the DVD cases were just for show. Most people would not have paid attention to them. A smart intruder would have noticed that there was no TV or DVD player.

That smart intruder would have found the disposable phone hidden in one of the cases. He turned it on, and put it with his regular phone. He would have to keep the old phone, because the police knew that number, and might try to contact him.

***

Sorenson always chose apartments near bus stops. He liked buses, not for environmental reasons, but because they were anonymous. The police could learn lots of things about his car, could find it with relatively little effort, could tail him easily if he drove somewhere. A taxi was less obviously connected to him, but it could be tailed even more easily, unless the driver was good and willing to help. And the cab firm would tell the police where he had been picked up and where he had gone, and when.

But a bus let him disappear in plain sight. He could get on here, get off there, and get on another one. Trailing someone who took a bus was almost impossible, and the bus company had no idea who was riding at any time, or where they got on, or where they got off. A really good tail might follow a bus, but he could get off and wait for another bus. A tail who was on the bus would stick out if it got off and waited with him, and lose him if it didn't. A tail following the bus in a car would almost never find a parking place at the bus stop.

He took a bus north for several blocks, watching out the back window for anyone following him. He hadn't seen anyone around the bus stop, but he wanted to be certain he wasn't being tailed. He got off the bus, crossed the street, and took a southbound bus three blocks past his apartment. The Golden Pub would be a good place to start asking questions.

The Golden Pub wasn't very golden. The paint had weathered into a dirty bronze color, and it hadn't been refreshed in a very long time. It was a pub, if you considered a pub as any place you could get a drink. If you thought it would be something quaint, English or Irish, you were going to be very disappointed. It was a small neighborhood bar with a purely local clientèle. It was not quite squalid, but close enough that strangers, though welcome, didn't stay long.

The people who hung out there didn't care about the appearance, or the grimy floor, or the filthy bathroom and its smells. They came to get a drink, to chat with their friends, and to kill a couple of hours after a tiring day at work. Some came to kill a couple of hours before a night of work. These were the people Sorenson wanted to talk to.

"Hey, Joe, is Ronnie here yet?" Sorenson asked the bartender before settling onto a stool at the bar.

"Yeah, he's in the can," said the bartender, "draining off the last two beers. Haven't seen you here in a while, been out of town?"

"No, just busy elsewhere," said Sorenson. "Pull me a Guinness, please. Have you seen Pete Peterson around lately?"

"Haven't you heard? Pete's dead," said Joe. "They found him dead in his own apartment this morning, shot. I can't figure that one out. Pete was careful about the jobs he took, and about who was around him. And as far as I know, he wasn't doing anything big lately. I haven't seen him in a couple of weeks, though, so I may be little out of date."

Sorenson looked up to see Ronnie coming from the back of the bar, paid the bartender for his drink, and waved Ronnie over to a table away from the other patrons. Ronnie got himself another drink and sat down.

"Joe just told me about Pete Peterson," said Sorenson. "Do you know if Pete was working on anything, lately? He usually didn't play with guys tough enough to do a killing."

"I saw him a couple of days ago at Al's Diner," said Ronnie, "and asked him if he had anything for me to do for anyone. He said he was working a job, but didn't need any help just then. He didn't say what the job was, but I didn't expect him to. Even if you were in on the job, he wouldn't tell you anything more than you needed to know. He seemed pretty upbeat about it, though."

"Thanks," said Sorenson, "it just seems so unlike him to be mixed up in something dangerous. I'm cautious, but he could give me lessons in being careful. And he did, too. Any other rumors you might have heard lately?"

"No, but I've been out for a while with some stomach flu or something," said Ronnie. "I felt good enough to go to Al's that night, but got worse the next day. So I haven't been doing much listening lately. Sorry."

They talked for a while longer, and then Sorenson got up, said goodbye to Ronnie and Joe, and left the bar. The street lights were on, but the twilight still showed the few people walking up and down the street. No one attracted Sorenson's attention and he walked a block to Angie's

Tap. It was another small neighborhood bar, cleaner than the Golden Pub, and with more patrons.

"Angie, what are you doing here?" asked Sorenson. "Where's that bum of a husband of yours'?"

"He twisted his ankle the other day," said Angie behind the bar. "Says it hurts too much to stand here all night. I kidded him that he'd do anything for a night off, but Fred deserves a break once in a while. The last two nights are the first he's missed in five years. Where have you been? Thought maybe you'd fallen off the edge of the world."

"I've been around, but just not around here," said Sorenson. "Still got a bottle of that good German beer?"

"There's just two left from that case you gave us," said Angie. "I really shouldn't charge you for serving you your own beer."

"Fred understands," said Sorenson, "he did me a favor, and buying my beer back from him is a way of repaying the favor. Besides, I like to know there's someplace I can get it."

"Here you go," said Angie, "and thanks for the tip, too. Oh, I almost forgot and talking about not seeing you in so long should have reminded me. Lefty is in the booth at the back. He was asking about you earlier. He looked worried about something."

"Lefty always looks worried about something," said Sorenson. "But I'll stop by and talk to him. Thanks for the beer, Angie. Tell Fred to get well soon."

Hidden away in a corner of the back booth, Lefty was nursing a gin and tonic. He had the glum look of a man who had never had a good day in his life. Sorenson knew better, knew how often Lefty had very good days, and how well he could arrange a good day if he wanted one badly enough. Lefty looked up as Sorenson sat down, and half-smiled.

"Angie said you were asking about me," said Sorenson. "Was it anything in particular, or just a general concern for my well-being?"

"Pete Peterson's dead, if you haven't heard yet," said Lefty. "And I've heard that some people are looking for you. I don't know who's looking for you, only that they don't want to buy you a drink. Is there any connection?"

"There might be," said Sorenson. "That's what I'm trying to find out now. I had done a small job for Pete, one so small it didn't really need to be done. It was obvious that there was more to it than my bit, and they must have killed Pete because he knew who paid him. I wasn't sure if they were going to come after me since I only knew Pete paid me. But they might not have known him well enough to know how tight he was with information. Where did you hear about these guys?"

"At Melissa's a couple of hours ago," said Lefty. "Some guy I don't know was asking about you, and not in a friendly tone of voice. No one volunteered any info on you, of course. Mainly because you haven't been there in what, four or five months? You might consider taking a little trip somewhere with a nicer climate."

"Yeah, things do seem to be getting warm around here," said Sorenson. "I know a nice little town in Maine where no one will think to find me. It's a little early to look at the fall foliage, but it's pretty, quiet, and I know a very friendly lady there. See you around, Lefty, and thanks for the warning."

Sorenson walked to the front of the bar, waved good-bye to Angie, and went out into the night time street. The street lights were dim along here, but he didn't see anybody waiting for him. His late lunch had carried him through the evening so far, but he was beginning to think of dinner. Melissa's wasn't too far to walk, and he could get a decent meal there, as well as anything else he might want.

***

The day had been warmer than expected, and the evening was still very comfortable, with no wind to make it cool. He walked at a steady pace, quickly enough to get somewhere without wasting time, but not so fast as to attract attention. He continued his contemplation of his current situation.

People are definitely after me, then. That is not good. It means death, of course, but it also means that I'm involved in something bigger than I imagined. A simple burglary, even of a police officer's house, should not require anyone to be killed. And certainly not everyone connected to it. What is really going on here? What had been hidden in that fireplace, and why is it so important?

Who did Peterson know who might be behind something this big? I know most of the people Pete knew, and I can't think of anyone who would kill to cover up a crime. Did Peterson know anybody that rough? And, if he did, would he have worked for him? The questions keep piling up, and they aren't attracting any answers. Maybe Melissa can give me a hint.

Melissa's place was in a large old-fashioned building, four stories tall, on the corner of two not-quite-busy streets. From the outside, it might have been an office building at one time. It had the look, inside, of a former hotel. It had a nice, moderately large lobby, with many plush chairs. There were a number of people lounging in the lobby, mostly men.

By the street entrance was a bar, opening off the lobby, with a few customers drinking and talking together. Next to the bar was a restaurant, also opening off the lobby. It was late enough that the restaurant was not crowded, but there were still a few diners lingering over their brandies. On the other side of the lobby was a grand staircase, possibly marble, going up to the second floor.

A careful observer sitting in the lobby all evening would have noticed the large number of people, almost all men, going up the grand staircase. An attractive woman stood at the head of the stairs, looking over the lobby. He couldn't decide if she was wearing a nice evening gown, or a very nice nightgown. Considering where she was, it could be either.

Sorenson could never figure out how Melissa could run a successful brothel these days, what with competition from so many street corner whores, a few high-priced call girls, and a city full of amateurs offering everything for free. He half suspected that she ran some respectable business, a candy shop, maybe, from the back room.

Sorenson walked through the lobby past the bar, and went into the restaurant. Unusually for this part of town, there was a maitre d' waiting for him. He was following the maitre d' to a table across the room when he heard a sultry voice stopping them.

"I'll take care of our guest, Paul," said Melissa in a velvety contralto. "We'll eat in my private room. Send in Pierre to wait on us. Come on, Jack, it's good to see you again."

They went into a room off to one side of the main dining room. There were three other similar rooms for private dining, assignations, and political plotting. They were private only in part. Everyone could see who went into a room, but no one could know what happened inside. The walls were well insulated to hold the secrets in.

Melissa chatted lightly with Sorenson while he read the menu and the waiter took his order, lamb chops, peas, and noodles. The waiter had just left when another arrived with a large stein filled with dark beer.

"I remembered what you drank," said Melissa, "though I shouldn't have, it's been so long since you've been here. It's good to see you again. You should stop by more often, even if you don't want to go upstairs. And a little stair climbing wouldn't do you any harm, either. I've got some new girls that might interest even your picky taste."

"I've told you often enough, Melissa," said Sorenson, "that it isn't the quality of your girls that keeps me away. It's that they are paid girls. I've never heard of any complaints from them about you, and I know you keep the rough crowd away from here. But a girl who screws men only for money isn't giving her all to the job. I prefer a girl who wants to screw me because she **wants** to screw me. She puts her whole heart into it, and that makes it a lot more fun for both of us."

"Ah, you're another romantic, in your own way, just like Peterson," said Melissa. "You heard about him, I suppose, or you wouldn't be here tonight."

"Yes," said Sorenson, "I was at the police station when the officers who found him brought in their report. I had a long conversation with some very nice detectives about it, too. I couldn't tell them much, because I don't know much. I saw Lefty a little bit ago, and he says he heard someone here asking for me, and not in a nice way."

"I didn't see Lefty," said Melissa, "but Dan the bartender saw him eavesdropping on some tough guy asking about you. Dan says he recognized the guy. Dan used to work at the Dead End Bar, you know what a reputation that place had. Dan was glad to leave there after only a couple of months, but he remembers faces well. He says this guy used to work for Roscoe."

A knock on the door announced Pierre with Sorenson's dinner. He quickly set the table, and placed the food in front of Sorenson. After being told that another beer was not needed now, he made a short bow to both Sorenson and Melissa, and left.

"Roscoe Queen?" asked Sorenson. "I didn't know he was still around. I had heard that he got a stiff sentence out East somewhere for a laundry list of felonies. I had also heard that he fled the country to avoid arrest for that list. And someone said he was dead, though I'll only believe that when I go to the wake."

"He's not dead," said Melissa, "but either of the other stories is possible. I've heard both of them, too, but no one seems to know which is true. But he does seem to be back in town. Rivera the dip says he saw him, or someone who looks just like him, at the airport last night."

"Last night? That's interesting," said Sorenson. "Do you know what time?"

"No, but I can have someone find Rivera and ask him," said Melissa. "Do you think Roscoe killed Peterson? Peterson knew better than to work for someone like Roscoe. And if Roscoe only arrived in town last night, how would he have found Pete so fast?"

"If Mr. Queen is involved, I think he had someone else setting things up for him before he got here," said Sorenson. "His subordinate was the person whom Pete dealt with, and probably the one who killed Pete. In a way, this almost explains part of the mystery.

"Mr. Queen took a strong dislike to Peterson and me a long time ago. We both turned him down on a particularly nasty job he wanted done, shortly before he left town. He threatened to kill us for refusing to work for him. We were concerned, but then he was gone and we stopped worrying. But if he's back and connected to this, he might have set us up just to get revenge finally. He needed something done here and may have picked Pete and me as his cat's paws. Have us work for him unwittingly, and then get rid of us. That would certainly suit his ego and blood lust."

"You need help, I can see that," said Melissa, "what exactly do you need? A hideout? A gun? An escape to somewhere else?"

"I don't use guns," said Sorenson, "I thought you knew that."

"I do, but even people who don't use guns can change their minds when the game gets too rough."

"Peterson was shot in the back of the head," said Sorenson, quietly, with a sadness for his friend. "A gun doesn't help if the killer is behind you and you don't know it. No, what I need is information. I know you have one of the best networks of ears in town. Between the girls upstairs who listen to their clients' babble and the street girls who are hoping to get promoted up to here (yeah, I know about them), you have access to more secrets than the FBI and the CIA combined.

"What I want to know is the identity of anyone who was planning to burgle a house belonging to a police officer. The choice of target has to make this burglary stand out. Maybe Mr. Queen's deputy kept it under cover too well. Maybe he did the job himself, or brought in outside help. But if anyone in town knows about it, I'd like to know. And I also want to know where Mr. Queen is now."

"You know you're asking for more trouble using his last name like that," said Melissa. "You remember what he did to that guy that called him 'Queenie'."

"No, nobody knows what he did to that guy," said Sorenson, "because no one ever found that guy. If I remember correctly, they never found the guy who noticed the first guy had disappeared, either.   But 'Queen' is his last name. And if he wants me dead now, he can't kill me any more dead for using his proper last name.

"Look, if it was just me in danger, I would probably just clear out for a while. I told Lefty I might go up to Maine to see the changing leaves. But someone killed Pete Peterson. And Pete was a good friend of mine. I don't like people killing my friends. And the police think I'm involved in this more than I've admitted. I could make some friends with them if I give them Mr. Queen on a platter. And save my own neck, too. So, ask your girls to listen for anyone talking about burgling a policeman's house."

"That's a long shot, you know," said Melissa. "Burglars aren't my usual clientèle, but the girls on the street may have heard something. And how did you know about them, anyway?"

"I never said you had a monopoly on learning secrets," laughed Sorenson. "I learn lots of things, some of them useful to me, some not. I could tell you an interesting story about the deputy head of the aquarium and the chief auditor of the car dealers association. It's a great secret, but it's not useful to me, or anyone else. I'll come in tomorrow night for dinner to see what you've been able to find out. Thanks for your help, past and current, and, I hope, future."

"Take care of yourself, Jack," said Melissa. "Pete was a very careful man and still not careful enough."

"I am exceptionally aware of that," said Sorenson. "It gives me the willies. Thanks, again."

Chapter Seven

Thinking about it later, when all the excitement was over, when he realized he was safe and in one piece, Sorenson credited the beer with saving his life. He had had three beers over the last two hours, and his bladder was complaining. Before leaving Melissa's place, he went through the door marked "MEN" and relieved himself, sighing the sigh that accompanies a long whiz.

Stepping out of the front door of Melissa's and onto the sidewalk, he spotted two things. The first was a big vehicle, a Ford Expedition, just pulling up to the curb almost across the street from him. The second was another car, a small, battered old Chevy, pulling out from the curb, further down his side of the street. The Chevy roared down the street, gaining speed like a drag racer, and aiming straight at him. Before he could react, the Ford pulled out from the curb and turned toward him also.

The Ford SUV wasn't moving as fast as the Chevy, but it only had to move across the street and it had a lot of mass. It rammed the Chevy's side hard, pushing it away from Sorenson. Sorenson jumped back in alarm, reacting late but still in time to avoid to being hit by either car.

The Chevy's momentum carried it across the sidewalk and it crashed into the side of Melissa's place. The old stone building took little damage, but the front of the car was badly buckled. The driver, dazed, struggled out of the passenger side of the Chevy and started running back up the street.

The driver of the Expedition was already out of his car, pulling a gun from a shoulder holster, and yelling "Freeze!" in a loud, imperative voice. The driver of the Chevy was only twenty feet away and eager to put more distance between himself and the other man. He pulled out his own gun and fired two shots wildly down the street.

He had hoped the shots would make the other man take cover, giving himself time to get further up the street. The Ford's driver, however, was calmly standing still, bracing his gun with both hands, and taking careful aim. His bullet caught the Chevy's driver in the knee and brought him down with a cry of great pain.

Sorenson looked at the SUV's driver and recognized him finally as the plain-clothes police officer who had tailed him home last night. The policeman went carefully over to the man on the ground, kicked his gun from his hand, and picked it up by the barrel. Back at his vehicle, he reached in through the window and pulled a radio handset out. After talking to someone on the other end, he came over to Sorenson.

"Thanks a lot," said Sorenson, "I wasn't expecting an ambush quite so soon. If I had come out a little bit sooner, you wouldn't have been here, and I'd be the one on the ground."

"Sorry I wasn't here a little sooner. My name's Markham, Sergeant Markham," he said. "Detective Mahoney heard rumors about people looking for you. Ten minutes ago he told me to check for you here. How did he know you'd be here?"

"Detective Mahoney's a good detective," said Sorenson, "he knows how people think and act. He only met me yesterday, but he already knows, without asking me, where I'd go to get information. What I want to know is how *that* guy knew I'd be here. The only guy who mentioned Melissa's to me wouldn't give me up as fast as that. I wonder if one of her people is taking a second paycheck from someone else."

A squad and an ambulance arrived almost simultaneously in a blur of flashing lights and sirens. The driver of the Chevy had alternated cries of anguish with curses and threats against Sergeant Markham. The paramedics from the ambulance moved him onto a body board, not gently, which caused him to stop cursing and concentrate on yelling in pain.

While the paramedics loaded their patient into the ambulance, Detective Mahoney arrived. He got out of his car and surveyed the scene slowly, taking in the two cars, the injured man, the other cops already there, and Sorenson. After talking with Markham and the two uniformed men, he went over to where Sorenson was standing.

"I don't know if I should curse you out for the long hours I'm putting in," he said, "or thank you for the overtime. I suppose you know nothing about this at all, as usual. It doesn't matter, we're going back downtown for another pointless conversation anyway. Hope it doesn't mess up your plans for the evening, not that I really care."

"I was actually through with my plans for the evening," said Sorenson. "And I want to thank you for seeing that I wasn't through

permanently. Sergeant Markham said you told him to look for me here –
that proves you are as good as I said you were. And you're wrong about
what I know and will tell you. Let's get where we can talk freely. I feel
exposed out here on the pavement."

***

To Sorenson's surprise, Mahoney led him to a walled cubicle near
the interrogation rooms. Mahoney pushed a wheeled office chair to
Sorenson, got them both ceramic mugs of coffee, and flopped down into
his own chair. Sorenson tasted the coffee and found it to be rather decent,
brewed in a pot, not a coffee dispenser.

Mahoney's desk held a computer monitor, a land line telephone, a
picture of a pleasant looking woman, a picture of two children, and just
short of a thousand pieces of paper. Most of the paper was arranged in
nice neat piles, but small scraps with names and numbers were all over the
desktop.

"A guy who does us favors told me earlier about people looking for
you." said Mahoney. "He didn't recognize them, or know who they were
working for. He said he saw two guys, and a friend of his said he saw
another one. The snitch said they were asking for where you lived, what
bars you went to, where you might be right then. They gave no reason for
their curiosity, of course, and they didn't actually threaten you, but the
snitch figured they weren't your friends. That's what I know, what do you
know?"

"Roscoe Queen is apparently back in town," said Sorenson. "That's
the big bone. It would satisfy a lot of your partners here, but I know you
want the whole story, and I'll give it to you. If Mr. Queen is here, and
looking for me, I need to leave town immediately or get him arrested even
faster. Here's the history of Pete and me and Mr. Queen.

"Several years ago, right before he left town, he had a big bank job
planned. Pete and I didn't do anything that criminal. Even taking a small
part like lookout makes you an accomplice, so we never considered
anything like that. We were in a coffee shop one day when Mr. Queen
comes in with some of his muscle. He sits down at our table and tells us

he wants us to do a job for him. I don't know why he wanted us, maybe he figured a couple of fixers were expendable.

"Even before he tells us what it is, I'm trying to find a safe way to say no. Then he drops the bomb, literally. He wants us to plant a couple of bombs at two grade schools on the far side of town. He figures the blasts will draw off all the police, and he'll be able to waltz in and out of the bank. Pete and I are scared white. There's no way we can do this, and there's no way he's going to let us beg off, now that we know what's going to go down.

"Well, before we have to say anything, a couple of beat patrolmen come in for some coffee. Mr. Queen looks uneasy, his men shift uncomfortably, and Pete and I take advantage of the slight diversion to jump up and run out of the place. We ran into the next store and hid. Mr. Queen and his thugs ran down the street and never looked at the nearest hiding spot.

"We made an anonymous call to police headquarters about the bank job and the bombs, because we didn't know if he'd find somebody else to plant them. I guess he couldn't find anyone to do that part, so the policemen watching the schools had nothing. But the bank was well covered, and your men almost got him that day."

"Oh, yeah, the Third City Bank job," said Mahoney, with interest and admiration. "So you were the guys who tipped us off on that one? The chief wanted to give you a medal for your help. Two cops got wounded, but not badly, and four of Roscoe's gunmen went down, two dead. Roscoe got away, unfortunately, but his gang here was destroyed."

"Yeah, and he seems to have figured out the part Pete and I played in that." said Sorenson. "I was surprised he went ahead with the bank job, but I guess he thought we'd be too afraid of him to squeal on him. But we were more afraid of letting him bomb some schools. We didn't know he'd give that up, and we had to tell the whole story if we were going to tell anything. So his opinion of himself as the toughest guy around blinded him to the risk.

"Afterwards, with his gang smashed and himself on the run, he probably figured out who finked on him. But he had no way then to get back at us. We heard he was in trouble out East, in jail or on the lam again, and stopped worrying about him. Now it looks like he's back and it's payback time. He found some way to hire Peterson for the fake kidnapping, with me as an additional cat's paw to tie up Inspector Radcliffe.

"Pete wouldn't have knowingly worked for Mr. Queen, so there's some other intermediary. We knew this morning he was working for someone else, now we know that's just a link to Mr. Queen. The link may have been the one who shot Pete, or maybe someone else. Maybe the guy who tried to run me down can fill in some more."

"If you had told us all of this earlier, you might have had a less adventurous evening," said Mahoney.

"I didn't know Mr. Queen was back and looking for me," said Sorenson. "And I didn't really know that until ten minutes before the adventure started. I'm willing to work all the way with you now for two reasons. One, I don't like it that a friend of mine was killed. Two, I don't like it that I might get killed, too."

"Revenge and survival," said Mahoney, "I'll take those as good reasons to help us. What about you, now? Do you want us to put you up somewhere safe?"

"Melissa's should have been safe," said Sorenson. "I've got a nice safe apartment, well-stocked with food and beer. I can hide out there for a while. You have my phone number if you need me."

"We've got a man watching your apartment," said Mahoney, "but your address is no secret. We can only spare one cop to watch you, and he can't cover front and back at the same time. Let us put you up somewhere else."

"You can call off the policeman watching that apartment," said Sorenson. "I told you I had more than one address. I'm staying at one now that even Pete didn't know about. Unless someone who knows me as Jack Sorenson sees me going in, I'll be invisible there. But I would like a ride home, it's getting late and the buses out my way don't run all night."

"If we give you a ride home, we'll know where you live," said Mahoney. "And we could be followed leaving here, so they will also know where you live."

"Only if you drop me off at my front door," said Sorenson. "Sergeant Markham was sharp at spotting that hit and run car before it could hit me, and he had only just arrived. If he's that good at noticing a tail, he can take me home. He can drive me down my street, and I won't tell him which street it is, drop me off a few blocks away, and I can walk home down alleys. Peterson was right in a way, knowing how to move like a spy is useful."

***

A light rain was falling as Markham drove Sorenson through the city. Sorenson noted with approval the way Markham watched his mirrors, made unnecessary turns, and doubled back from time to time. He was sure that no one was going to follow them all the way back to his neighborhood, much less to his door. Even so, he gave a few more wrong turns to cloud the trail further. When they finally reached his street, he gave no sign of paying special attention to it, but he looked carefully at every doorway and parked car. Four more turns, and three blocks away, he told Markham to let him out.

He watched Markham drive off before going into an alley across the street. Honest people stayed away from alleys, especially at night, and especially dark, rainy nights. Sorenson found them reassuring. Holdup men might hang out at the mouth of an alley, but not on a wet night. And the length of an alley was usually empty of people, except for the homeless, and they weren't going to attack him. And someone following him would stand out in an empty alley much more than on an almost empty street.

There were boxes, some with people sleeping in them, dead to the world, unaware of his passage. There were other boxes filled with trash, and garbage cans, all pushed back along the walls Alleys never got much traffic, but the middle of an alley was always empty, open to any vehicles that might come through. And the middle of the alley was just far enough from the walls to give him warning of attack from a hidden assailant.

There wouldn't be any assailants tonight, he knew, because he had been careful, and because Sergeant Markham was good. Still, practice was good, and he needed to stay alert after the scare outside Melissa's brothel. Mr. Queen was a very dangerous man, possibly psychotic, certainly considering himself above any law and any rules. Sorenson had to assume that for the next several days, at least, he was going to be risking his life going out at all.

That might become a problem. He had three clients lined up for cash deliveries on Monday. They wouldn't like it if he didn't show up. He wouldn't like to miss his commissions, either. But he would be too exposed if he were to try to do these jobs. And he couldn't ask Peterson to cover for him anymore.

The alley crossed a busy street, well lit with bright street lights and neon signs on some of the stores. He looked up and down the street and saw no one lingering in any doorways. When there was a break in the traffic, he darted across the street and into the alley opposite. A peek around the corner revealed no movement on the street. Safe again.

Two more streets, not as well lit or traveled, and he was onto his own street. There was still no sign of life on the streets, and he strolled casually past his own building. He stopped to tie his shoe lace, looking one last time for a sign of a follower, or a watcher. Then he went back to his door and went in. Leaving the lights off in his apartment, he peeked out the window. Still no one. Still safe.

His phone rang.

"Jack, Melissa here. I just heard from Rivera. He was at Midway airport last night and saw Roscoe about half past eleven. Does that help any?"

"Yes, it definitely does. Thanks a lot, Melissa. I appreciate the help."

He undressed in the dark and crawled into bed. It had been a long day, up too early with Mahoney's visit, too many hours at the police station, too much time walking from bar to bar, too much of a scare at Melissa's. He was tired. He was very tired. He was ......

***

Whitey McGraw was a thug. He had always been a thug. He had no other ambition in life but to be a thug. He worked as a thug for Louie Pasquale. He was tough. He was dependable. He was not terribly bright. But thugs didn't have to be bright. They just had to be tough. Now he was in trouble.

Louie Pasquale was not a thug. He was Roscoe Queen's right-hand man, and the only member of the gang who ever dared disagree with his boss. At five feet eight inches tall and one hundred sixty pounds he was not imposing to look at, but he had a steely gaze that few others could stare down. He was the self-styled brains of the gang, and most of his plans had worked out well for them.   Just now he was trying to control Roscoe's temper.

Roscoe Queen was a large man, six feet four inches tall, two hundred fifty pounds, and all muscle. In his youth he had been a weight lifter when he wasn't committing crimes. As his criminal life grew, his interest in body building slackened, but never quite disappeared. He liked to be able to beat up anyone he wanted, anytime he wanted. He used a gun as a matter of course, and a knife sometimes. But he preferred to beat people into submission.

His temper was never entirely under control and even his closest associates were afraid of angering him. Associates, not friends. He had no friends. No one was completely comfortable around him, because he might blow up at any moment, with or without a reason. Right now, he felt he had reason.

"Look, Roscoe, I understand you're upset," said Louie nervously. "But we were together all the time. We put the stuff in the fireplace together, and Whitey held the board while I mortared the bricks in place. You were watching. We left and spent the night with the gang, going over the plans for the bank job. We were all together at the bank, and we all got away together. We've all been within a block of each other practically ever since leaving this burg. When could he have taken the stuff?"

"All I know is that you two put the stuff in there and sealed it up," said Roscoe ominously, "and now it's gone. No one else knew where we hid the stuff. Whitey had the newspaper article about the robbery. I wanted that to show any buyers we found. And he dropped it into the bottom of the fireplace. Accidentally, he says. So I had him make a note about the article with the date and the paper.   And he lost it, he says. Accidentally, he says. He says he set it down on the mantle. He thinks maybe it fell in with the mortar. Did you see it in the mortar? I didn't. I think he found his own buyer.

"Everybody else in that gang is dead or in jail. And the guys in jail only know we took the jewels, not where we hid them. That was just the three of us. And if someone else had found it by accident, the news would have made the papers, even in Philly. This was a big haul. We break open the fireplace and the hole is empty. How can this be?"

"Roscoe, if Whitey had taken the stuff," said Louie, "would he have come back here knowing the hole was empty, and knowing how mad you'd be? I don't think he's suicidal. He knows you'd kill anyone who double-crossed you. He's helped bury some of them. I don't know what happened. He don't know where the stuff is. I don't know where the stuff is. We've both been with you forever. I trust him. He's never tried to work his own angles, or cheat you. Who told you about that guy who …."

"Sorry, Louie," said Roscoe, "I can't trust him any more. You know what that means."

Roscoe was standing so close to him, Whitey didn't even see him edge the gun out of his pocket. The shot was loud, and fatal. The next five were just to let Roscoe vent his anger.

***

Thursday morning was bright and sunny, with not a cloud in the sky. Birds would have been chirping outside his window if he lived in a less urban neighborhood. Sorenson looked at his watch and sighed. Ten o'clock already. He had come in well after midnight. He must have been more tired than he had thought.

Most of the morning gone and he was still in bed. Well, it didn't matter. He couldn't go anywhere or do anything anyway. He got up, showered, and made breakfast. He thought about taking a chance and going out for a newspaper. Then he realized that his most important problem was just a minor note to newspaper editors. If they knew the whole story, it would be on page one. But the continuing investigation into Peterson's death wouldn't get much coverage.

He took a book from one of the shelves. *Kim*, by Rudyard Kipling, a story of a young boy learning spy craft in colonial India. Peterson swore by it as a guide, and Sorenson liked the way the boy tried to balance his spy life and his non-spy life. Sorenson never felt the pull of a normal life, but he still had to pretend that he had one. The pretense was his camouflage, like Kim's lama, a show of normalcy to cover something very un-normal.

Chapter Eight

"You're here early," said Mahoney Thursday morning. "Get to bed nice and early since you didn't have to finish your watch here?"

"Yeah, like that was going to happen," grumbled Radcliffe. "I told you I was going to go talk to my realtor. And then I had dinner. And then I cleaned up the living room. And if you think that got me to bed early, you're not half the detective I think you are. But it was not without benefit.

"Here's a list of the previous owners of the house, with dates of purchase. Run the names through the database and see if anyone has any connections to major criminals. Actually, give this job to Sweeney, with a copy of the list, he's clever with the database files. I want you to take on the tougher part of the job.

"Track down each of the buyers and learn whatever you can about them. Ages, current residence, occupations, why they bought this house and why they sold it. Start with the last one, Rodriguez, the one the bank foreclosed on. The bank may be able to help you with him. By the time you've checked him out, Sweeney may have more addresses for you.

'Find out, too, how long the house may have sat empty between owners. Donaldson sold in 2009. Did he have too much debt after the mortgage meltdown? Was the house empty before whosit, Falkenberg, bought it? We don't know when the thing was planted in the house, but if they built a box for it, and waited to fill the box, the house was either empty for a long while, or the owner was in on the crime.

"One more meaningless clue. I was just finishing the clean-up when I found this on the mantle piece. It wasn't there before the break-in, and it's not Paul's handwriting nor mine, and there was mortar sticking to it. Check to see if it's a phone number. Give the name to Sweeney, too, one more won't strain him. Don't wait for him to run the name, though. Check out the number, then try to think of something besides a phone number that it might be."

"Good thing I came in early, too," said Mahoney. "Well, only some of it will require miracles, so I guess I can handle it. And here's my wizard to help me now. How's it going, Sweeney?"

"Morning, Inspector," said Sweeney to Radcliffe. "It's going just swimmingly so far, Sam. Here's your list of criminal bricklayers and masons. There's twenty of them, but some of them haven't practiced the trade for years. Anything else you need this morning?"

Mahoney gave him the list of house buyers and the name from the scrap of paper, and told him what he wanted, and Sweeney promised him results in full by early afternoon. Mahoney then left for the bank that had handled the foreclosure.

***

Phyllis Radcliffe sat down at her desk and glowered at all the other cases she was working on, in neat piles scattered all over her desk. *Some of these are important, but my case is important, too. Someone involved with it has been killed, that makes it important. That makes it Paul's case, actually. Still, he has only the murder half, I still have the burglary half.*

And the burglary half includes Mr. Starp. Who is he? Maybe Sweeney could provide an answer to that soon. But what sort of name is Starp? I've been on the force long enough to learn most of the ethnic names in town, and the neighboring towns, as well. And Starp doesn't ring any bells.

Maybe it isn't a full name. Maybe it's a shortened name, like Pete for Peterson. Starpovich? Starponsky? Starpiola? A nickname, maybe, and god only knew how he might have gotten a nickname so odd. But people did sometimes have odd nicknames. My brother used to be called Dant, for Daniel Taranski.

Well, then, could Starp be Star P? Star sounds like a girl's name. The gun moll. Ugh. She was definitely reading too much Raymond Chandler and Dashiell Hammett. Her meditations were interrupted by a familiar voice.

"Can I talk to you for a minute, Phyllis?" asked Paul "This case keeps getting more complicated."

"I came in early to get a jump on the clues I have to follow up on," said Phyllis, "what are you doing here now? Your shift doesn't start until four."

"How long have we been married? And how long have I been on the Homicide Squad? You know very well my shift starts when they find the body. They were polite today, and didn't call me in until I had just finished breakfast.

"Some garbage men hoisting up a dumpster found a body behind it this morning. It belonged to Whitey McGraw, who used to work for Roscoe Queen. Neither one has been seen in town since the Third City Bank job, years ago. I only mention this to you because Mr. McGraw had brick and mortar dust on his clothes."

"What the hell!" exclaimed Phyllis. "How does a serious criminal like Queen get tied into a house burglary? Okay, the burglars were after something hidden in the fireplace, and that could be something big that a big-time crook like Roscoe stole. Sam Mahoney and I figured that out already. If Roscoe Queen is involved, we should be able to find some big unsolved crime from several years ago and be able to find a connection."

"That's a good theory," said Paul. "You weren't a detective when Roscoe left town, and I was just a junior one. We'll have to talk to some of the older guys about this, and search the case files. Where's Mahoney, he might have an idea?"

"I sent him out looking for wild geese," said Phyllis. "A list of prior owners of the house I got from our realtor, and a name on a brand new unfathomable clue. I found this on the mantle last night when I was cleaning up."

"Starp? What kind of name is that?" asked Paul.

"That's what I was trying to figure out when you came in," said Phyllis.

"Well, I'll put it in the back of my mind," said Paul. "The front is too full of Whitey McGraw. He didn't just work for Roscoe, he was one of his chief henchman. They stuck together like they were joined at the hip. It doesn't make much sense for Roscoe to kill him. And it doesn't make much more sense for someone else to kill him and make Roscoe mad."

"Do you think it will be useful to question Sorenson again?" asked Phyllis. "He's like a magic orange, every time we squeeze him, we get a little more juice."

"You can, if you want to," said Paul. "I've got to get back to the homicide end of this case. Let me know if you find out anything from him, or Mahoney, or any of your other leads."

***

"I'd like to talk to you again, Mr. Sorenson," said Phyllis. "I have some new information, and I'd like to hear if you have any comments about it."

"I doubt if I can add anything," said Sorenson, "but I've committed myself to helping the police solve this case. Not out of civic duty, but from a sense of self-preservation. I'll be there by two-thirty."

***

Mahoney and Sorenson arrived at Phyllis' office at the same time. She had just finished crossing off the last name on the list of crooked bricklayers. Five of the twenty had died, six more were serving long sentences in prison, six more had moved out of state years ago. The remaining three were too old to be of interest.

Sorenson took a seat while Phyllis briefed Mahoney on her search. Mahoney then gave a rundown on the buyers.

"Fred Johnson was the original owner," said Mahoney. "He'd been there for decades, sold to move to a retirement home. He died there in 2007. Morgan bought the place as an investment property. Fix it up, turn it around, and sell it for a nice profit. Which he did to Mr. Reisler, who had the same idea. And the same result. He added the fireplace, or rather, he expanded the fireplace to its current size. He seems clean, but since he did work on the fireplace, I've got Sweeney digging a little deeper.

"The big fireplace appealed to Mr. Donaldson, who paid way too much for it, and the rest of the house. He was seriously under water, as they say, when the housing bubble burst. He couldn't meet the mortgage payments and moved to Peoria, where he had another home. He put this one on the market, hoping to get enough to cover his mortgage. He finally did, that fireplace appealed to a lot of people, apparently. But the house was on the market, and empty, for several months. Donaldson almost defaulted on it, but he got out almost whole.

"Mr. Falkenberg bought it from Donaldson, and kept it for three years. He liked the house, he told me over the phone, but he got transferred to Miami and had to sell. Mr. Hoover's wife was the first person who didn't like the fireplace, and she finally made him sell the place to get rid of it. Rodriguez was the only crook in the lot, as far as I can see. He was caught embezzling from his boss, and went to prison. The bank foreclosed when he stopped making payments. That's where you come in."

"So the only long stretch when the house stood empty was when Donaldson was trying to sell it," said Phyllis.

"Long stretch, yeah," said Mahoney, "but some of these guys said there might have been a week or two, maybe more, between sale and occupation. So the fireplace might have been set up any time."

"No, it was while Mr. Donaldson was trying to sell," said Sorenson from the back of the room.

"How can you possibly know that?" asked Mahoney with exasperation. "You keep coming in here, giving us the slimmest answers to any questions we ask you, and then dropping information from out in left field on us. Have you ever met any of these people before? Have you even heard their names before? If you're holding out on us again, I'll nail your hide to the side of city hall."

"I saw Mr. Falkenberg's name," said Sorenson, "on a scrap of paper I pulled from Peterson's hidey-hole. I told you about it yesterday, but no one followed up on it right away. I got there a few hours after I mentioned it to you, and found the scrap in the hole. Here it is, a real, live clue, just for you. Just the name Falkenberg. I didn't know who it was until just now."

"So how did Peterson come to know this name?" asked Phyllis. "If he knew nothing about the crime's details, how could he know this?"

"I don't know,' said Sorenson, "but maybe his contact was a little careless and mentioned it. Maybe he thought of the house as the Falkenberg house, not the Radcliffe house. Your guess is as good as mine."

"Okay, then, what can you tell me about Whitey McGraw?" asked Phyllis.

"Nothing pleasant," said Sorenson. "He's a thug for Louie Pasquale, Roscoe Queen's right-hand man. Roscoe Queen seems to be back in town. If Roscoe Queen is here, so is Louie Pasquale, and so is Whitey McGraw. He used to hang out at Biff Tollandson's bar, if you want to find him."

"No, we can just go down to the morgue if we want to find him," said Phyllis. "He got thoroughly ventilated last night and dumped in an alley. Paul's adding him to his collection of dead people associated with this crime."

"House burglary is a little tame for Whitey McGraw, not to mention Roscoe Queen," said Sorenson. "Are you sure he's connected?"

"His clothes were covered in brick and mortar dust," said Phyllis. "That seems to pull him in. Any ideas on why two big-time boys like these would be breaking and entering an ordinary house?"

"It's only an ordinary house to you, the owner," said Sorenson. "Or any of the other owners. To the criminals, possibly Messrs. Queen, Pasquale, and McGraw, your house is not a house, it is a vault. An especially useful vault, because only they can see it as a vault. To everyone else, it is just a house."

"Are you after my job?" said Mahoney with wonder. "Did you really just figure all that out sitting here, just now?"

"No, I don't want your job," said Sorenson. "Right now, staying alive is the hardest work I've done in years. You have to do real work every day. I couldn't take it. But I told you I read crime stories for fun. You've seen the house, I presume. I haven't. In your mind you see a physical form that matches what you've actually seen. To me it has no real form, it is just a mental concept. So I can envision it in all sorts of ways. Something was hidden in it; that makes me think of vaults. So the house is a vault.

"If Mr. Queen, or someone else, stole something really valuable that he had to hide for a long while, walling it up in a fireplace is a good idea. No one will look there, or even think of looking there. Probably none of the people on the list had any connection to the crime. This house just happened to be available at the right time, so they used it."

"So what was hidden there?" asked Mahoney. "I know you don't know, but you're making a lot of good guesses. I'd like to run your string a little longer. How much could it be worth? Yesterday Phyllis and I figured at least 100 grand. Does that sound reasonable to you?"

"Too little," said Sorenson. "I got $15,000, and Pete may have gotten more."

"He could have been shot instead of being paid," said Mahoney.

"No, this is a cash only business, in advance," said Sorenson. "Pete had his share up front. He probably paid me a share of his share. And he wouldn't have left it lying around his apartment, either. You mentioned something like that yesterday, and I should have corrected you then. When we get paid, the money goes into the bank just as soon as possible. Then there's the expense of faking the surveillance tapes – not a lot, but something. Even if it's just Messrs. Queen and Pasquale, the thing has to be worth enough to make it worth coming back for.

"If Pete got, say, $30,000 for his share, which is the low end of my guess, based on what I got, they've paid out $45,000 for this thing. It's got to be worth much more than $100,000, especially to guys at their end of the scale. I would guess, and I am really guessing here, guess at least $250,000, and probably over half a million."

"Wow!" whistled Mahoney, "Really?"

"I said it's just a guess," said Sorenson. "You've seen the hole in the fireplace, I haven't. How big a thing could fit into it? A large satchel full of money? A bag full of jewels – compact and valuable? A piece of expensive art? Size and value aren't always related. I saw a story about a small painting about the size of a postcard, what they call a miniature, selling for two million bucks. I've never heard of Mr. Queen going into art theft, but there's always a first time. But I don't really have any more idea than either of you do."

"Well, then try your brain on this one," said Phyllis. "I found this on the mantle piece when I cleaned up the mess last night. It wasn't there before the crime, so the criminals must have left it. But there was mortar on it, so it may have fallen out of the fireplace. Can you decipher it? Do you know anyone named Starp? He's not in our databases."

"Starp1102109? Starp?" asked Sorenson. "What kind of name is that? I have even less of an idea on this one. May I copy this and think about it? I'm hiding out and have time to spend on interesting puzzles."

"Sure, make a copy," said Mahoney. "I'll give you a picture of the fireplace and the box we found inside it. I'm almost beginning to like working with you – you're clever, and you think fast. More important, I'm starting to think you're not holding out on us."

"You were right to begin with," said Sorenson. "I was holding out information about Peterson's part in what went down. But after he was killed, I've given you everything I know. Oh, wait, I forgot one thing. We've been talking about him and I still forgot. Mr. Queen was seen at Midway airport Tuesday night by a pickpocket named Rivera, about eleven-thirty. Melissa told me that, and in the excitement of almost being killed, it slipped my mind. But if Mr. Queen was coming in on a late flight, maybe that's why you had to be out of the house until two in the morning."

"Well, that's possible," said Phyllis, "and it makes sense, too. Not that much about this does make sense. It would help if we knew what they were after."

"And why someone killed Whitey," said Mahoney. "That part still makes no sense. Go home, Sorenson, and think deep thoughts. If you figure it out and embarrass me, I'll thank you from the bottom of my heart. Because I doubt if anyone can solve this one."

Chapter Nine

Sorenson took five buses to get home, just to be certain he wasn't being followed. He lost one suspicious fellow, not a policeman, after he left the second bus. *I don't like it that someone had been on two buses with me. But the tail is definitely gone. I'll have to change the pattern of buses to avoid having someone waiting for me at the third stop. This is indeed getting to be too much work. The payoff, staying alive, is worth it, of course, but I still don't like the job.*

My usual job is so easy, and actually fun, most of the time. Delivering envelopes full of money is simple, and surprisingly safe. No one knows I'm carrying large amounts of cash, so no one tries to rob me. The women are mostly attractive, sometimes pleasant to talk to, and only occasionally interested in taking me to bed. That would be bad if the sugar daddy found out, and he would, somehow. But I figured out a long time ago how to deflect unwanted attentions.

The bookies are professional and business-like. They aren't actually polite, but they aren't rude to paying customers, or their agents. The others I deliver money to are at least cordial, happy to be paid. Even the pol whose drunken wife I take to the clinic – he may not like dealing with me, but he treats me well enough that I won't go to the press and embarrass him.

I can come and go as I please all month long. Only on the first of the month am I obliged to be anywhere and do anything. A few hours work delivering envelopes and I have the rest of the month off. Unless another job comes up, which often happens. More work means more money. And few jobs cut into my free time that much.

Time to wander the streets, in a car, on a bus, on foot. Berwyn, Cicero, Chicago, Oak Park, all the whole metropolitan area if I want. It's not possible to know too much about your surroundings. I had a great time learning the tunnels under the Loop, all open to the public, and all unknown. And very useful knowledge when I had to give that bookie's bodyguard the slip. Stupid bookie shouldn't mind paying off the winners. If he doesn't, they won't come back and lose.

Time to read books, books on almost any subject. That book on the Athenian navy was very interesting, and well written. I ought to check out some more books on Greek history. It might be a worthwhile new topic.

*Time for going to the movies, and the theater. I should take Marcy to that new play at the Chicago Shakespeare Theater. Not now, of course, but when this mess is over. She'll like it, I think. Time for Marcy, theater or no theater. Not a wife. Not a mistress. She's her own woman, and I like that about her. Would she ever be interested in marriage? Could **I** ever be interested in marriage? Hmmm, enough introspection. I'm getting hungry.*

He had told Melissa he would dine with her again tonight, but last night's attempt on his life made him cancel. *I probably wouldn't be attacked there twice in two nights, but why take chances.* And there were good restaurants in this neighborhood. Berwyn was a good town for eating out, whatever you had a taste for.

He had dinner in a restaurant two doors down from his apartment. He had a decent and authentic goulash made by a Mexican cook. The Mexican cook had been trained by the Hungarian owner of the restaurant. The Hungarian owner had sold and was now long settled in the outer suburbs. The ethnic neighborhoods were changing, but sometimes bits and pieces like this survived. And sometimes they merged with the newcomers, like the CzechMex Goulash Taco also on the menu.

The street was still free of loafers, watchers, and other suspicious types. Sorenson slipped into his doorway and went up to his apartment. He closed the drapes before turning on the lights and poured himself a beer. Time to think some more.

If Roscoe Queen is involved, whatever had been stolen must have been stolen before he fled town after the Third City Bank job. How long before? No way to tell. Mr. Queen is a hasty man, quick to act, quick to anger, but he does understand that some loot appreciates over time. Picasso never got the kind of money his paintings sold for nowadays. Of course, Mr. Queen isn't Picasso, and doesn't normally steal art works. But even jewels could be worth more to a fence after the heat had died down.

And jewelry would fit nicely in the box in the picture. A boxed diamond necklace, or ruby, or emerald. A stack of boxes. A bag of bracelets, brooches, unboxed necklaces. With the right stones, a small package could be worth a very large amount. But I'm wasting my time guessing about what was in the fireplace. The police could print out a long list of unsolved robberies that I've never heard of. Leave that part to them.

What could be done with the other clue? Starp1102109. What could that be? Is Starp a name? A nickname? A person or a place? What is the number referring to? It isn't a phone number, I'm certain of that. I've created enough fake identities to know that a phone number can't begin with a "0" or a 1." So is it an address? Not around here, too many digits. Even on the far south side of Chicago, 170th Street would give an address of, say, 17056.

Well, could it be a combination? Two parts of an address run together. Maybe 110th Street, apartment 2109? Or 110 109th Street, apartment 2? How many ways could I play with these numbers to get a possible address? Possible as an address, and possible as a way of writing down an address. I need to check the Chicago Phone Book. The maps in it might give me a hint.

He went to the bureau drawer where he kept the phone books for Chicago and all the near suburbs. He had a set in every apartment, just in case he needed one. They sat, unused, almost all year long, but once in a while they were useful. As he pulled out the large first volume, he noticed the paper lining the drawer was torn. *I should replace it, but I don't have any newspaper to put in its place.*

His mother had always lined her bureau drawers with newspapers, though he had never known why she bothered. Probably because her mother had done it. And he did the same, from the same habit. The wood of the drawer was not going to contaminate the clothes or other objects put into the drawer, so why bother? Habit. He'd take out the old piece of newspaper and leave it out to remind him to replace it. It had been there for a long while, the Village Star, dated February 4, 2011. He took the phone book to his chair and sat down again and thought.

The Star wasn't published anymore, gone four years ago. Too much of its income was derived from the store ads for Sears, and Penney's, and other big stores. As they closed stores, they cut back their advertising, and that starved out the small local papers. It was a shame, and not just for the people working there. It was the only source for local news for the people of Berwyn, Cicero, Oak Park, and the others.

The Sun-Times or the Tribune would tell you what happened around the world, but almost nothing about what happened around the corner from you. There was that fire at Maginty's Bar and Grill. Front page of the Star, and a small paragraph in the Tribune, page ten, with Maginty's name misspelled. Ah, the good old Star.

The Star. The Star. The Star, Page 1. Starp1. Starp1102109. Star, Page 1, 102109. Star, Page 1, 10/21/09. The Star, Page 1, October 21, 2009. Could that be it? Could it be that simple? No, it wasn't simple. If I hadn't seen the paper lining the drawer, I wouldn't have thought of it. How can I find out if it means anything?

If the Star were still being published, I could go down to its office and someone could go through their morgue to find the page. The public library used to carry it, and might still have a copy in some archive somewhere. Or maybe on microfiche. But the library is already closed for the night. It might be archived online somewhere, too, but that means going out.

He never used the internet from any place connected to him. He knew how to use a computer, but always used one at the library or an internet cafe. Secrecy was more important than convenience in his work.

Should I call Inspector Radcliffe or Detective Mahoney? No, not until I know I'm right. If it turned out to mean something else, I don't want them thinking I'm muddying the waters. They still aren't sure I'm helping them enough. It was almost 8 o'clock anyway. They should be going home soon. It could wait until the morning.

There was an internet cafe three blocks west and four blocks north. Alleys all the way. I really should check it out tonight. If I'm wrong, I won't waste the night thinking about what I might find tomorrow. If I'm right, I can spend the night thinking about, well, whatever it is.

Sorenson picked up a walking stick from the corner by the door. It was just an ordinary walking stick, no hidden sword blade (the police would not like that), no hidden gun (the police would like that even less), but it was hefty. It was made from solid oak and had a round solid brass head. And he knew how to use it in several very interesting ways.

Nothing would protect him from a bullet fired at a distance. But against a gun up close, well, he might have a chance to disarm the gunman.

***

The internet cafe was not crowded tonight. A kid playing some online action game, a couple of teen-aged girls giggling over someone's Facebook page, a man researching butterflies. In fact, he had never seen it crowded, and wondered absently about how they managed to pay the bills. What really went on in the back room? What customer information was sold to whom? He didn't care, he never left anything traceable to himself on their computers.

The Star's website was still online, supported by some advertising for dating sites, and a former publisher reluctant to bury his departed love. He logged in using John Smith's highly useful identity and opened the Search window. He had used the website before and liked the results – full page images of the paper, not just a few headlines. He typed in the date, October 21, 2009, and waited for the front page to appear.

The big headline was "Barziger Collapses, Election Uncertain." Big local news, now forgotten. And since when is the re-election of the local party boss ever uncertain. But there was another story just below the fold that attracted Sorenson's eye.

"Crown Jewels Stolen"

In a daring daylight robbery, five men broke
into the Stiplitz Museum yesterday and stole
the Crown Jewels of Albania, including
the Royal Crown, the Orb and the Scepter.

Well, that's something that will fit easily into a fireplace hiding spot. The crown and the orb would probably fit into the box. It would depend on their size, and the photo doesn't give dimensions. Still, the crown is tall. Crown? It looks like a medieval helmet, with a horned goat head on top. Good journalism, everyone would want to see a picture of the Crown Jewels. Must have been a tight fit in that box. The orb, a shiny ball with a double-headed eagle on top. The scepter, some sort of staff with the same eagle on top. Hand held, so not too long. Maybe they stood it on end next to the box.

So, just like that, the puzzle is solved. Oh, right, just this part of the puzzle. What it was is important, but even more so is where it is now. If Mr. Queen stole the Crown Jewels and has reclaimed them now, he took them because he now has a buyer for them. In a few days at most, the jewels will be hidden away again, in some private collection, no doubt. Time to go home and think about possible buyers.

***

Stepping out onto the sidewalk, Sorenson noticed a white van drive past, and the passenger looking out the window. The van was rather ordinary, but the passenger was definitely Mr. Roscoe Queen. Sorenson wasn't sure if Mr. Queen had seen him. The van didn't turn around. But caution suggested taking a bus home. Alleys might suddenly become dangerous.

The bus arrived a couple of minutes later and followed in the wake of the white van for a few blocks. Sorenson lost track of the van before he even got on the bus, but he kept his eyes open for any sight of it, or of Mr. Queen. It was because he was looking out the window that he saw the kidnapping.

***

Another ghastly day that lasted much longer than it needed to, thought Phyllis Radcliffe as she left Paul's office. *So the bullet that killed Peterson was not from the same gun that was used to kill Whitey. Roscoe used to have lots of henchmen, presumably he still had lots of them. Go home and rest. Have a little whiskey and wait for Paul to come home.*

Her thoughts, as she walked across the parking lot, were interrupted at this point by a man in a Dodgers jacket, quite out of place in a Chicago suburb. Then she saw the gun. He held it discreetly close to his body, but the barrel was very much in view, and pointed at her.

"Don't give me any trouble, lady," he said softly but menacingly, "just come along quietly."

He pushed her lightly down the lot, away from her car and toward an ambulance. Before she had taken more than three steps, she was simultaneously surrounded by two other men who grabbed her arms. They hustled her quickly toward the back of the ambulance.

***

Sorenson saw a woman being dragged across the police department parking lot by three men. She was struggling against all of them, with some success. He saw one man go to his knees after her foot connected with his crotch. One of the other men slapped her face hard, turning it toward him, and he recognized Phyllis Radcliffe.

The bus had only slowed for a traffic light, but not come to a stop. Now it was moving away from the parking lot, and Sorenson could see no more. But he already had his phone out, dialing 911.

"I've just witnessed a kidnapping in the police department parking lot," he told the operator. "The victim is Detective Inspector Phyllis Radcliffe. She was being manhandled into an ambulance marked Kwik-Evac. I'm on a bus, and it's moving. So I can't tell you which way the ambulance is going to go. Get a squad out now."

As he spoke, Sorenson was pulling the emergency cord to stop the bus. The driver snarled back, "Wait for the next stop, buddy."

"I'm going to be sick," moaned Sorenson convincingly, bringing the bus to an immediate stop.

Works every time, thought Sorenson as he jogged back to the police station. There was a lot of commotion in the parking lot, and Sorenson spotted Paul Radcliffe in the middle of it.

"I'm the one who called in the kidnapping," said Sorenson. "I don't know if he did it, but I saw Roscoe Queen in a white van heading this way just a little before it happened."

"You again," said Paul in exasperation, "why is it always you again? Wait, I'm sorry. [Deep breath] Thanks for calling in when you saw it. We got a squad out after it before it had gone a block. The chase is still on."

"Look for the ambulance to be abandoned soon," said Sorenson. "I think they'll transfer to the white van as soon as they can. If your squad keeps the chase tight, they may not be able to do that, but that's what I would expect."

"License number?" asked Paul, hoping.

"No, I didn't know it was important until later," answered Sorenson. "It was just a plain white Ford van. Half the small businesses in town have them for deliveries or tools."

"I wish you hadn't said Roscoe Queen," said Paul. "Any policeman is willing to face some danger as a part of his job. I am. Phyllis is. And I am willing to let her face that danger – it's her choice of work. But no man is comfortable knowing his wife is in the hands of a beast like Roscoe Queen. Why would he want to kidnap my wife?"

"For the same reason he broke into your house, I think," said Sorenson. "But it doesn't make sense, not this part. I think I know what he took from your fireplace, but if he's got it, he should be leaving you two alone."

"Inspector, there's a radio report just in," said a uniformed cop, "the squad lost the ambulance. But we've got a half dozen squads in that area, and will try to pick it up again."

"Have them look for a white Ford panel van, also," said Paul. "The kidnappers may have switched over to it.

"Let's go inside," said Paul, "there's no sense in standing out in the parking lot any more."

***

"Would you like some coffee?" asked Paul as they entered his office. "Freshly brewed for the end of the shift. Though this shift may last a lot longer than normal."

"I'd prefer a beer just about now, but considering department rules, I'll settle for coffee," said Sorenson.

"So, you think you know why Roscoe broke into my house?" asked Paul. "You said earlier that you had no idea what was there, or even if Roscoe was involved."

"True," said Sorenson, "but Detective Mahoney asked me to go home and think deep thoughts. He was being snarky, a bit, but that's what I did. And I accidentally found the link that connects all, or anyway, most of the questions we have. I was reminded about the old town newspaper, the Star, and something clicked in my mind."

"Hold on," said Paul, as his personal phone rang. "Yes, this is he, uh huh, yes, who are you? I'd like to speak to her. Just let me hear her voice. What? I don't know what you want. We don't have anything of yours. If it was in the fireplace, someone else took it. I can't give you something that I don't know about, or where it is. Look…

"They hung up. That was the kidnappers. They want the stuff that was in the fireplace. They didn't tell me what it was, but they assumed we had it. What was it? You said you've got an idea about it."

"Starp wasn't the name of a person, it was part of a reference. Star, the newspaper, page 1, 10/21/09. I was out at an internet cafe checking it out when I saw Mr. Queen. The important story that day for us was about the theft of the Albanian Crown Jewels from a museum."

"Albanian Crown Jewels?" yelled Paul. "What the hell! Does Albania even have crown jewels? And how did we get involved?"

"The article did mention that there was a kingdom of Albania in the 1930s," said Sorenson. "Mussolini invaded Albania and seized the jewels. After the war they disappeared for a while. Finally someone brought them to the States, and donated them to the museum.

"It's the sort of big target that Mr. Queen would go for. And it's the sort of attention-grabbing loot that would have to cool off before he could sell it for what he wanted. Somehow he found out about the empty Donaldson house and decided to use the fireplace as his vault. Now he wants the money and goes to retrieve the jewels. Having them, he should be disappearing, not attracting attention with another kidnapping. I'm lost again."

"But he doesn't have them," said Paul. "And if Roscoe doesn't have the jewels, and I don't have the jewels, who does have them? And how did he get hold of them? And what has he done with them?"

"The last question is easy," said Sorenson. "He sold them to someone. He obviously got them from the fireplace, but how he found out about that hiding place is anybody's guess. And who is even harder. Maybe if we knew who he was, we'd be able to figure out how he knew. Or vice-versa, if we knew how he knew about the hole, we'd be able to figure out who he is."

"Will Queen hurt Phyllis?" asked Paul quietly. "Everyone knows his reputation for violence and brutality. What will he do to her?"

"His reputation is well-earned," said Sorenson, "and I suspect he will have already beaten her to get her to tell him where the jewels are. Since she couldn't tell him, he called you. Since you couldn't tell him, he'll probably beat her some more. He likes beating people, but he's not overly stupid. He knows it will do him no good to kill someone who is the only one to have the information he wants."

"That doesn't explain Whitey, though," said Mahoney from the doorway. "I heard about Phyllis and my wife said if I didn't come back here and find her, she'd divorce me. But if Roscoe did this job, Louie Pasquale would have been in on it. Whitey was Louie's thug more than Roscoe's, but he would also have known where the loot was, and he was in exile with Roscoe. If Whitey found some way to steal the stuff before Roscoe came back, and Roscoe suspected Whitey, then, yeah, Roscoe kills Whitey, but not before finding out where the stuff is."

"Yeah, if Whitey took it, he'd tell where it was, trying to save his life," said Paul. "And if he didn't take it, why kill him? As you say, even if Roscoe just thinks Whitey cheated him, he'd want to know where the stuff was before killing him."

"And if Whitey didn't have it but knew how it had disappeared," said Mahoney, "he would have told Roscoe that."

"Maybe Mr. Queen is getting more unstable," said Sorenson. "He was always somewhat psychotic, a danger to friend and foe alike. He never liked not getting his way. Maybe he blamed Mr. McGraw not for stealing the jewels, but for somehow letting someone else find out about them.

"Someone else is involved. Someone who had no connection to the robbery, nor to Mr. Queen, nor, probably, to you, Inspector. Someone who found the jewels by accident and kept them, or, more likely, sold them. The mysterious Mister X, who always shows up in the last chapter of cheap detective novels to confess to everything."

"How do we find him?" asked Paul, "do we just skip ahead to the end of the book and peek?"

"No, you're going to have to do it the old-fashioned way," said Sorenson. "You and Detective Mahoney and a whole lot of other police officers are going to have to pound the pavement, dig into your databases, interrogate huge numbers of people who know nothing about anything. You know, the usual police routine. You have the staff, and the training, to find the answer to this question. I'd start by going back to the owners after Mr. Donaldson, and asking them some more questions."

"Like about the fireplace?" suggested Mahoney. "And anything unusual that might have happened to it?"

"That would be a good place to start," said Sorenson.

***

Roscoe nursed his injured hand. It was still bleeding from the first punch into Phyllis' stomach. He had hit her large metal belt buckle and sliced a gash across the back of his knuckles. Now it hurt him to punch her almost as much as it hurt her. This shouldn't be. He shouldn't be pulling his punches. He shouldn't flinch in front of his men.

"Leroy," he said, "I'm doing more damage to my hand than to her. You take over, and don't be easy on her. Cowboy, get me that rag in your jacket pocket to wrap around my hand before I bleed to death."

"That's a nasty gash, Roscoe," said Cowboy, "but you ain't goin' to bleed to death from it. And that ain't a rag, that there's a pocket handkerchief. It came with this jacket when I stole it. It makes me look distinguished."

"Distinguished my ass," said Roscoe, "it makes you look like a jerk."

Cowboy felt insulted, but he didn't dare complain to Roscoe. Even at six feet two inches and two hundred pounds he wasn't about to challenge the boss. He liked the blazer he had taken the year before, even if it didn't give him a tough guy image.

Hernando was holding Phyllis by the arms, keeping her on her feet while Leroy punched her. He was six feet tall and one hundred ninety pounds, tall enough and strong enough to hold her up without any trouble. He came from Texas and looked like a Mexican bandido, with a bristly mustache. But his family had been in Texas since before the Alamo.

"Come on, lady, talk!" said Roscoe. "I don't have all night. Tell us where the stuff is, and tell us now!"

"I don't know what you're talking about," gasped Phyllis. "What stuff?"

"The stuff that was in your house," roared Roscoe. "Tell us where it is and I'll let you go."

"What stuff?" asked Phyllis.

"Hit her some more," yelled Roscoe. "Keep pounding her until she talks."

Leroy was a wiry five feet six inches tall and one hundred forty pounds. He had been a professional boxer in his younger days, and still kept in practice. He was the smallest of the gang, and needed to be able to handle any of the others, except, of course, Roscoe. He knew how to throw a solid, damaging punch.

He also knew how to throw a fight, making good looking punches that fooled the audience, but did no harm to his opponent. And he didn't like the idea of beating up a woman, even a cop. She would be bruised when he was done, but not as badly as if Roscoe had done the job.

Half an hour later, with interruptions for more unanswered questions, Leroy threw a hard punch that knocked Phyllis out of Hernando's grasp. He knelt beside her and whispered, "Stay down."

"I'm getting wore out, boss" Leroy told Roscoe, "and she's passed out. Let's give it up."

"She don't know nothin', boss," said Cowboy, "either that or she just likes gettin' beat up. I know bimbos that like that, but she don't look the type. Tie her up and leave her here, and let's go."

"No," said Roscoe, "she must know something about it. She and her husband must have been the ones that found it."

"But boss," said Louie, "they're cops. If they had found it, they would have turned it in for the reward. Or they would have sold it and retired. We would have heard about it if it was returned. And if they sold it, they wouldn't still be cops. She says they've only lived there two years. That leaves almost seven years for someone else to have found it."

"Okay, then, just kill her," said Roscoe, "and let's get out of here."

"Boss, what are you thinkin'?" blurted Cowboy. "Kidnappin' a cop is one thing. Killin' one is another. They will never stop lookin' for you if you kill her. She says people have seen you in town, so they'll come lookin' for you. They don't know me, and I can disappear easily. But they want you for lots of other crimes, already. Add a cop killin', and your days are over."

"I don't like wimps," said Roscoe. "I especially don't like having wimps working for me. I tolerate you right now only because Whitey is no longer here, and I need guys to do things for me. You can join him, if you want. Now, get in the car. Leroy, shoot her and join us."

As Roscoe went out to the car, he heard a gunshot behind him, and he smiled.

Chapter Ten

Bright and early Friday morning, Mahoney was calling Mr. Arthur Falkenberg in Miami.

"Hello, Mr. Falkenberg, my name is Detective Sam Mahoney, of the Berwyn Police Department. We talked yesterday about a house you used to own here in Berwyn. Yesterday I was only looking for some basic information about your purchase and sale of the house. I now have some more detailed questions for you. We are investigating a burglary that happened here recently at that house. We believe that at some point before you owned the house, somebody hid some stolen items in the house."

"How unusual," said Mr. Falkenberg, "I find that hard to believe. My wife and I completely remodeled the interior of the house. We didn't tear down every wall, but we did some rearranging of the walls. I'm certain that if something had been hidden, we would have found it."

"We believe that the stolen items were hidden in the fireplace," said Mahoney. "As part of the burglary, the fireplace was broken into, and a secret compartment was discovered. Did you do any work on the fireplace in your remodeling?"

"Oh, no, the fireplace was one thing we thought was perfect," said Mr. Falkenberg. "But you say the stolen items were hidden there before we bought the house? And they were just recently removed, so why are you calling me?"

"I'm sorry, Mr. Falkenberg," said Mahoney, "I was not very clear about this. Let me try to explain this again. Sometime in 2009, before you bought the house, several stolen items were hidden in the fireplace. It was then repaired to look normal. In 2016 the house was sold to its current owners. They had no idea anything had ever been hidden in the fireplace. At some point during those seven years, the items seem to have been removed. We think that someone found the items by accident and kept or sold them.

"We aren't accusing you, of course. We are just trying to find out if anything unusual had happened to the fireplace, something that would have let some third party find the items and remove them. We are looking for any remodeling of the fireplace, or perhaps repair to some damage.

Anything which would allow a third party, a bricklayer, for example, to work on the fireplace. But if you did nothing with the fireplace, I'll have to check with some of the later buyers of the house. Thank you for your time."

***

One down, two to go. Mahoney called Hoover's phone number and got his voice mail. He left a simple message to call him back, and looked up the number for Pablo Rodriguez. Rodriguez answered promptly and made things easy for Mahoney by being in the building, talking to his parole officer.

"Hello, Mr. Rodriguez, I'm Detective Mahoney," he said, coming into the parole officer's office. "I have a few simple questions for you. Nothing for you to worry about. You owned a house here on 16th Street a few years ago, and lost it in a foreclosure."

"Yes, I was having trouble with the mortgage," Rodriguez replied, "and I stole money from my employer to pay it off. It was stupid, and I got caught and put in jail. I'm trying to go straight now, just ask my parole officer, here."

"Yes, he's scared of going back inside," said the parole officer. "He's got a job now and never misses his appointment with me. I wish I had more parolees like him."

"What I'm interested in doesn't really concern you," said Mahoney. "That house was recently burgled. We believe the thieves were looking for some items of value which they had previously hidden there. That would have been years before you owned the house. We also believe the items were later removed by someone other than the original thieves. We know that you did not take the items, because their value would have cleared up your finances.

"What I want to know is this, did anything unusual happen involving the fireplace? Did you have any work done on it? Did it need to be repaired at any time?"

"No," said Rodriguez, "the fireplace was fine. I never used it, or anything, it was just something there in the living room. But I never did anything with it."

"Okay," said Mahoney, "thanks very much for your time. I appreciate your cooperation."

***

Hoover still hadn't called back. Mahoney looked at his notes and saw that Hoover owned a small business on Cermak.   Mr. Hoover might be busy running his business, and not worry about phone messages from strange cops. A little visit might speed up the investigation.

"Is Mr. Hoover in, please?" asked Mahoney of the receptionist. "My name is Detective Sam Mahoney, and I would like just a couple minutes of his time."

"He's pretty busy today, officer" said the receptionist, "we have to get a big shipment out by the end of the day. It's the end of the month. It's a day that's always crazy busy.   Could he call you tomorrow?"

"Jane, has Potter got those shipping orders ready yet," said Mr. Hoover, coming out of his office and seeing Mahoney. "Who are you? Doesn't matter, I have no time for salesmen today. Come back tomorrow, or Monday."

"My name is Detective Sam Mahoney, and I would like exactly two minutes of your time. I talked to you yesterday about a house you used to own on 16th Street. We now believe that, sometime before you owned the house, some criminals hid their loot in the fireplace of the house. The house was recently burgled and the fireplace smashed open, revealing a hiding place.

"The criminals have now kidnapped one of the current owners, demanding the return of their loot. The current owners know nothing about the loot, so it seems to have disappeared before they bought the house. My question to you is , did anything unusual ever happen to the fireplace while you lived there?

"Well, nothing serious," said Hoover, "I rather wish something had happened to it. I liked the house, but my wife hated the fireplace. I told you we finally sold the house because she hated the fireplace so much. The only thing that ever happened to it was the lightning strike. Even that didn't destroy it."

"What happened?" asked Mahoney.

"The house got hit on the chimney by a pretty big bolt of lightning," said Hoover. "It broke up the chimney pots, and somehow cracked the brickwork of the fireplace. We had it repaired, but my wife still hated it."

"Do you recall when this was?" asked Mahoney. "And do you recall who did the repair work?"

"It was about five years ago, I think, in, um, July of 2013," said Hoover. "There was a big thunderstorm. I can't remember who did the work. I just picked a name from the phone book. My wife is home, now, and she can look at my check registers to find his name. Jane, give Mary a call to tell her Detective Mahoney is coming. I'm sorry, Detective, but I really have to get back to work."

"That's quite all right, sir," said Mahoney, "you've been very helpful."

***

Mary Hoover was waiting on the porch for Mahoney, and asked if he'd like a glass of lemonade as she brought him inside.

"Thank you, Mrs. Hoover," he said, "I'd like that very much. Did your husband's secretary tell you why I've come here?"

"Oh, she's not a secretary, she's the receptionist," said Mary Hoover. "She actually does all the work of both, but her mother told her to never be some man's secretary – he'd be forever chasing her around his desk. It's kind of a joke between us. Dennis is too afraid of my temper to even think of chasing her, or any other woman, and he's too afraid of losing her, too. She's very competent. Now, what was it that you wanted? She just told me something about check registers."

"Yes," said Mahoney, sipping his lemonade. "Mr. Hoover said that when you owned the house on 16th Street, the fireplace had been damaged by lightning. He paid for the repairs with a check, and I'd like to know who did the repairs."

"Oh, that fireplace," snorted Mary Hoover, "I hated that thing. I hated it when we bought the house, but Dennis said it would grow on me. He wanted the house, and it was a nice enough house. But that fireplace! It had the ugliest color bricks you could imagine. And it didn't look any better after it was repaired, either. I made Dennis sell the house just to get rid of that fireplace. Now, let's see, that would have been in 2013, I think."

"Your husband thought it was July of 2013," said Mahoney.

"Oh, yes, here's the check register," said Mary Hoover. "May, June, July, ah, here it is. Fireplace repair, check to Mr. Ralph Stevens. Do you need to know the amount?"

"No, ma'am," said Mahoney, "the name is all l need. Thank you very much for your help, and for the lemonade."

***

Finally, a name, thought Mahoney. *A real, identifiable name. A name with a real person attached to it. Of course, Mr. Ralph Stevens is probably long gone from Berwyn, and from Illinois. Maybe even the country. Well, he is not likely to be a career criminal, so he will not be skilled in hiding his tracks. Finding the jewels will be difficult. He must have sold them immediately, and the buyer may have sold them again to a collector.*

The jewels are not my problem, however. Roscoe might want them in exchange for Phyllis, but that will never happen. Why doesn't Roscoe understand that? The museum will want them back, too. And the insurance company, if they were insured. Still, not my problem. Right now, all I have to do is find Mr. Ralph Stevens.

"Sweeney," Mahoney bellowed when he got back to his office, "I need your wizardry again."

"You could learn to do these searches yourself, you know," said Sweeney, sauntering in casually. "I teach a class for cops who need to do digital searches. Internet, internal databases, FBI, Interpol, the whole ball of wax."

"Yes, but then you would be out of a job," said Mahoney. "And I would be wasting my valuable time doing badly what you can do so well, and faster. It's called division of labor, and it makes the world go round smoothly.

"See if you can find me anything at all, here or anywhere, about a man named Ralph Stevens. He was a fireplace repairman, or maybe just a bricklayer, around here in 2013. He probably left town sometime in July of that year, or a little later. Look for large amounts going into his bank account, well, you know what to look for. I don't think he's a professional crook, if that helps any."

"It might," said Sweeney, "amateurs often leave more obvious trails behind. On the other hand, none of the police forces in the world will ever have heard of him. I'll get right on it."

***

Many police departments won't allow an officer to work on a case if he has a personal connection to the crime. Someone else will hunt down the burglar who broke into your house, the purse snatcher who robbed your wife, the gunman who tried to kill you. A personal connection might make an officer think of vengeance, might make him focus too much on one suspect, might blind him to another. A rash pursuit of the wrong suspect was bad for the suspect, bad for solving the case, and also bad for the department's reputation.

In this case, the Chief of Police felt that a) Paul Radcliffe was one of the best investigators he had, b) that Radcliffe was professional enough not to lose control of himself, and c) that there was no way to keep Radcliffe from investigating the kidnapping of his wife short of locking him up. Besides, he felt that a little extra zeal would do no harm.

"Any news on Phyllis?" Paul asked as he came in at 8 AM, hours early for his normal 4 PM shift.

"No, Paul," said Michael Feltz, his lead detective, "not a thing today. They found the ambulance last night after you went home. It was empty, with no fingerprints except Phyllis'. No one saw a white van near the place. We've got the whole force out looking. The Chief says this is your case. I guess you decided that, too, coming in now. I wasn't going to wait, either. But we've got nothing to go on. All of Roscoe Queen's known hideouts date from nine years ago or more. Two places have been torn down, three more have changed owners and are now fairly clean."

"That won't slow Roscoe down any," said Paul, "he'll find an empty building, even an empty apartment, though not if he intends to beat Phyllis into talking. Have the boys check all the warehouses and empty storefronts. Any place he can hide and be brutal without attracting attention. Get cooperation from our neighbors, too. Mt. Auburn Cemetery and those parks next to the Stickney Water Reclamation plant are good places to hide outdoors, and they're close but not in Berwyn. Have we got the press in?"

"That started last night," said Feltz. "The morning local news are full of the story, with pictures of Phyllis and of Queen. No good responses yet, just 'my dog barked last night' and stuff like that. Every one of the neighboring towns is already working with us. But there's a lot of territory to cover. We haven't got a ghost town here, but there are a lot of empty houses, stores, and warehouses in the general area. And it doesn't have to be permanently empty. If he stumbles upon a house whose owner is on vacation, it's just as good."

"You're right," said Paul, "but thanks for getting all the bases covered right away. What about the guy who tried to run down Sorenson the other night? I suppose he's still in the hospital, but have you asked him where Roscoe is hiding out?"

"Not yet," said Feltz, "I was going there next."

                                    ***

MacNeal Hospital was large, the buildings and parking lots filling the whole block, with outbuildings for specialist care spilling over into the next block. Joe Brown was in room 343, his knee in a cast, and his mind full of pain. A policeman sat outside his door to ensure that he did not receive any unwanted visitors. Unwanted meant unwanted from the perspective of the police. Detective Feltz did not fall into that category and was waved in by the patrolman.

"Good morning, Mr. Brown, I am Detective Feltz. I would like to ask you some questions about some people we believe you are familiar with."

"Fuck you," said Brown, "I ain't talking to no cop. They read me my rights. I ain't gotta say nuthin' without a lawyer here. And I ain't gonna say nuthin', even with a lawyer. So there. You can't make me say nuthin' about nobody, no how."

"We're looking for Roscoe Queen," said Feltz. "You are currently charged with attempted murder. With your record, that could bring a very long sentence. If you were to cooperate with us, we could ask the prosecutor to suggest some leniency to the judge. Roscoe is going down, and when he does, he won't be able to hurt you. So why not help us bring him down?"

"Roscoe? I don't know no Roscoe," said Brown. "And if I did, I wouldn't squeal on him. I ain't a rat. So fuck off!"

***

"This kind of loot doesn't just disappear," roared Roscoe. "Someone took it, and they sold it. They didn't turn it in to the police, or we'd have heard about it. They didn't return it to the museum, or we'd have heard about it. They probably didn't keep it, because it looks valuable and is therefore worth money. And who doesn't want easy money? I want you to find out who bought it. Is that so hard? Just check the usual fences."

"OK, boss," said Louie, "but we've been away a long time. I ain't sure my list of fences is still good. Don't worry, I'll make a new list. I know how to find them. Hell, the small fences couldn't handle something like this anyway. And the big ones are probably still in business.

"Here's another idea, boss. We should look for the guy who took the stuff, too. Maybe he sold it to a private collector, and not to a fence. Maybe he sold it out of town. If the local fences didn't handle it, we'll need to find him, anyway. Let Hernando and Cowboy try to find him."

"Good idea, Louie," said Roscoe, "but where are they going to start?"

"We know that some guy named Falkenberg bought the empty house a month after we hid the stuff," said Louie. "They can start with him, and if he didn't take the loot, find out who bought the house after him.   There must have been somebody else before the cops bought the place. Hernando can put pressure on people pretty good. They'll find out who took the stuff."

"OK, you heard him, boys," said Roscoe, "get going and don't be too nice with anyone. Got it?"

Chapter Eleven

The Sacred Shrine was on the right hand wall of his office, close to his desk, where he could look at it easily whenever he wanted. Zef Tanush had debated mounting the pieces on a mannequin. *It would have looked more like a real king that way,* he thought. *But I'm not an artist, and I didn't want to hire an artist to create a life-like image for the figure. Today's artists, bah. Who can tell what they paint? And a blank mannequin face would just not do. I would have had to provide proper clothing for a realistic figure, and what clothing should it be? The ancient garb of my medieval ancestors? The modern uniform of the worthless King Zog?*

No, this arrangement is much better. The Crown on a glass shelf at eye level. The Orb of State on a glass shelf, just beneath the Crown. And the Scepter held horizontally by two small brackets under the Orb. It is neat, it displays all three pieces clearly and cleanly, without distraction. It satisfies me.

The Crown is unlike most crowns I've ever seen. It had been the helmet of Skanderbeg, the great Albanian hero, who fought against the Ottoman Empire. He had worn it proudly in many a battle. It is only proper that his helmet should be his crown. And the horned goat's head that decorates the top of the helmet/crown makes it distinctive, an object of great art, unique among crowns. It makes my home more Albanian, less modern.

My wife says the apartment is quite nice, elegant. It had been her choice, because the wife should have a house that pleases her. She likes the modern bare walls and the large area of the living room and dining room, open to each other. I would have preferred something which might have reminded me more of the old country, but I know that Albanian farmhouses are not a popular style for decoration in America.

To be honest, I have to admit that I would have had something like this even in Tirana, if we had stayed. Rich people do not live in farmhouses, and I want to live the life of a rich man. And I am certainly rich. This very plain apartment had cost over $800,000 ten years ago, and I was offered more than a million two months ago. But Ajola would *not move, even for money. She is right, money is not everything. A happy wife is.*

And could anyone but a rich man possess such a treasure as I have, right here. The ancient Crown of his ancestors, along with the Orb and Scepter. True, my personal ancestors had never been kings of Albania, but what difference does that make? King Zog had had no better claim, either. No one cares about royal ancestry these days, anyway. All that matters is that I have the Crown, the Orb, and the Scepter.

It had been the happiest day of my life when I had purchased the treasures from that strange American. Happier than my wedding day, happier than the births of my two children, happier even than coming to America and becoming rich.

How fortunate for me that I was in that antique shop that day. I had been looking hard for an anniversary present for my beloved wife, Ajola, and couldn't find anything I thought she would like. The American came in while I was looking at those over-priced bracelets, flashy but cheaply made, and not as old as the shopkeeper claimed.

The American had a large bag and had offered to sell the items in it to the antique dealer. The antique dealer had offered him a pittance for them, and the man was about to leave when I had seen them. I had often visited the Stiplitz Museum, and recognized the Crown and Orb immediately. My heart raced as I glimpsed the treasures I had so often desired.

I followed the man out into the street and stopped him. Would he sell to a private buyer? What price would I pay? God! What a question! What price did he want!? The conversation had been short and to the point, and the sale was agreed on without any haggling. My mother would have scolded me for not bargaining the price down, but my father would have been pleased that I had acquired so valuable a treasure at any price.

It had taken me a few days to raise the $1,000,000 the man had asked for, and I had worried that the man might have found another buyer. But my worries were unnecessary, and now it is all mine. The museum does not deserve to have such a treasure as this. It had not displayed the Crown Jewels properly, not even advertised their presence in the *collection. They had not appreciated the jewels. But my wife and I do, and every day we kneel before the shrine and offer incense and prayers for the future grandeur and glory of Albania. Our son and daughter, too, when they are home, join in the family ceremony. It is good to maintain ties to one's ancestral roots, even while living a very different life in a very different land.*

***

Ralph Stevens looked out the window at the men working on the pool, thinking: *It 's late enough in September to drain it for the winter and cover it over, but it's a shame it has to be done today. The weather is still warm, unseasonably so, and it's still tempting to spend another day or two swimming. No matter, the kids are back in college, and the wife has other plans for this weekend.*

Things were certainly going well these days, he thought. *It's not surprising that a bucket of money could make my life better. That's what money is for, isn't it? But it had done so much to improve all of their lives. Alice had stopped complaining about my lousy career. She was as loving now as when we had first married.*

And I can send the kids to college, something I had never thought I could do for them. They're bright kids and deserve a chance to get an education that will get them good jobs. They know they will have to make their own way in the world, that the money is for me and Alice. But I can at least give them a push in the right direction.

And all because of that crazy foreigner. I had barely understood the man at first, his English was so jumbled from excitement. But he had wanted to buy the stuff I had found in the fireplace, no questions asked. And he hadn't flinched at the price I had demanded. A cool million dollars, tax free because I didn't report it.

How could I? Technically, it was stolen, sort of. I didn't have anyone's permission to take it, but it had been sealed up in that fireplace for a long time. I doubt that anyone even remembered the stuff was still in there. But I knew that it could give us a new, better life. And now we've got it. A nicer house, a loving wife, two happy kids. All worth it.

***

"You are one lucky guy, Mahoney,' said Sweeney. "Your bird never flew. He lived in Chicago then and he lives in Chicago now. Here's his address, rather a nicer neighborhood than he left behind. I'm pretty sure it's the guy you want. He used to do chimney and fireplace repairs, and quit and moved in August of 2013."

"I guess I get to take a drive into the city, then," said Mahoney.

"Want me to call Chicago PD to cooperate with you?" asked Sweeney.

"No, I think I'll just be questioning Mr. Stevens now," said Mahoney. "If it becomes necessary to arrest him, then we can turn it over to them."

***

It was indeed a nice neighborhood, Mahoney noticed, and the address he wanted was the nicest of the bunch. The house was, of course, one of the ubiquitous Chicago bungalows. They had spread across the city and the near suburbs like a wave. This was a very nice bungalow, larger and more substantial than most. The lawn was perfect, almost like a golf course. Some of the flowers in the bed in front of the house were still in bloom.

A van for a pool cleaning outfit was parked out front, and he could see the workmen coming from the back of the house. He waited a bit and saw them get into their van and drive off. Time to call on Mr. Stevens.

"Mr. Ralph Stevens?" asked Mahoney of the man answering the door. "My name is Detective Sam Mahoney of the Berwyn Police Department. I would like to ask you a few questions about something that happened in July of 2013. May I come in and talk to you?"

"I don't know if I want to talk to you without a lawyer present," said Ralph nervously. "I don't want to be saying anything wrong to you and getting myself in trouble."

"I would like to make this a friendly conversation," said Mahoney. "I have no arrest warrant, no search warrant. My questions will involve your role in the removal of certain objects of value from a certain location. But we have not yet considered whether there was a crime connected with that removal. It's rather complicated.

"Please, let me ask my questions. If you don't want to answer any of them, just say so, and I'll go on to the next one. I don't want to have to get a warrant and arrest you, because your lawyer won't let you say anything then. Even if you only give me some answers, or even partial answers, I may learn what I want to know. I repeat, right now you are not considered a suspect in a crime. And yes, I'll be honest, that could change."

"All right, come on in," said Ralph, resignedly. "And I was just thinking about how wonderful my life was ever since I found those jewels."

"Thank you for saying that," said Mahoney, "it's easier to get the hard parts out right away. You found the objects in a fireplace you repaired for a Mr. Hoover, is that right?"

"I don't remember the guy's name," said Ralph, "but, there was a big crack in the fireplace. He said lightning had struck the chimney. I had to take a bunch of bricks out to do the repair work. How did you know I found the stuff? I never told anyone where I got it."

"The thieves who put it there came back for it," said Mahoney, "nine years after they left it. It wasn't there, of course, because you had it. We've been following the most invisible of clues to learn what we know so far. What you found was the Albanian Crown Jewels. Now, we'd like to find those jewels. That's why I'm here, to learn whom you sold them to. You quit your job and bought a nice house with a pool, so we know you sold them to someone. All I really want now is the name of the buyer.

"I can't tell you what your legal status is right now. You should talk to a criminal lawyer about it. Tell him everything you did, he'll need to know that to tell you where you stand. As far as the Berwyn Police Department is concerned, today, the jewels were stolen by somebody else. We think we know who, but we haven't the proof yet. The thieves hid the loot in Mr. Hoover's fireplace. It wasn't his fireplace, actually, since he bought the house later.

"You took the loot without Mr. Hoover's permission, but he did not know he had the jewels. Technically, that is theft, but he sold the house, and made no claims of robbery. Without a report of a crime, we cannot charge you with a crime. An ambitious prosecutor might try to charge you with possession of stolen property, but not if he has any sense. He couldn't prove that you knew it was stolen.

"Anyway, I don't want to arrest you, I just want to get the name of the man to whom you sold the crown and the rest."

"Are you, I mean the authorities in general," asked Ralph, "going to take everything I've got away from me?"

"Not for me to say," said Mahoney, "but I told you, right now you aren't being charged with anything. This case is so complicated that I don't think anyone will want to charge you with anything. The way it has developed, you are small potatoes, not worth the time and trouble to charge. I'm sorry if that sounds insulting, but you're better off that way."

"Well, then, I might as well tell you what I did," said Ralph. "I had to open up the fireplace to repair it. The crack was in the mortar, not the bricks, but I had to take a lot of bricks out to make the repair. And when I did, I saw this staff standing there, inside a hollow spot in the upper fireplace. It was all shiny and had big gems all over it.

"And there was a box next to it, with a small door. The door wasn't on hinges, it was just stuck into the opening of the box. There was no handle or knob to pull it open and I had to use my crowbar to open it. It fell off, down into the bottom of the fireplace.

"I looked into the box and saw this helmet with a goat's head on top, and a big sphere with a jeweled eagle on top of it. I took the things out and looked at them. I was utterly amazed. I had never seen such beautiful jewelry in my life. I knew it had to be worth a fortune. And I wanted that fortune. Things were tight, and Alice, my wife, was not happy with me. I could fix our troubles very easily if I just took the stuff.

"I figured it didn't belong to the guy who owned the house. It was a nice house, but not the sort of place you'd live in if you had a treasure like that. I didn't worry about who else might have owned it. It was mine now. I was only seeing dollar signs at that point.

"I put the things into a large bag, and went into Chicago, trying to find an antique dealer who'd buy them. No luck. No luck at all. I don't know if they thought the stuff was phony, or if they were afraid I'd stolen it and the cops would be after them. Anyway, no one wanted to touch the stuff.

"Then I left one antique shop and a guy who'd been in there came out after me. He was a foreigner, and he was so excited, he could hardly speak English straight. When he finally calmed down, he said he wanted to buy the things from me, no questions asked. I asked him how much he'd pay me. He asked me how much I wanted. God! What a question! I said a million dollars. He said OK.

"We met again a few days later, once he had got the money together. I gave him the bag of jewels, and he gave me a bag of money. We shook hands and we both left laughing. That is the whole story of how I sold the jewels. But the question you asked me is one I can't answer. I never asked the guy his name. I was so astonished that he agreed to give me a million that I never thought to ask. I'm sorry. Is this going to be bad for me?"

"Oh, god!" moaned Mahoney, "every time I get close, the finish line moves on me. You wouldn't believe how happy I was this morning when I learned your name. I thought I was finally going to find the jewels. And you forgot to ask the man his name.

"No, it's not going to be bad for you. You've been as cooperative as you could be. It's bad for me, because I have to go out looking for rich foreigners with crowns. Thank you, Mr. Stevens, you really have been helpful. It's not your fault you couldn't be more helpful. If someone gave me a million bucks, I'm not sure I'd ask his name, either."

Chapter Twelve

A policeman's worst day is not spent running around town tracking down suspects, looking for clues, trying to get statements out of witnesses. That kind of day keeps him so busy that he doesn't even notice the hours passing. He's worn out but he's not bored. He may be frustrated, but he knows he has done everything he could to find what he wanted.

The worst day is when he has no clues, no suspects, and no witnesses. When he has already asked everybody every question he can think of. When he has nothing to work with, even though he has a serious case to work on. Sitting in his office, waiting for a phone to ring or a witness to walk in, is slow torture. He can't make the time go faster, he can't make the break in the case just appear magically. And it was double torture for Paul Radcliffe, since it was his wife who was the victim of the crime.

He got briefed regularly by the sergeants running the search teams. He talked to the other departments, now all focused on this one case. It wasn't because they liked Paul, or Phyllis, it was because she was a police woman. She was one of the team. It didn't matter whether they knew her personally, or from her work, or at all. It didn't even matter that she was a woman. She was police. That was all they needed to hear.

But hearing that, and feeling the urgency of rescuing her, and giving every effort to find her, they still didn't find her. Hours passed with no news of her whereabouts. Every white panel Ford van in the area was checked out, and its owner questioned. There was no sign of Phyllis Radcliffe or her kidnappers anywhere.

About two in the afternoon, driving down a side street on the south side of town, Sergeant Doyle told Saunders, his driver, to stop. He had spotted something lying on the ground and wanted to get a better look at it. He walked over and saw a large sign face down in the alley. He picked it up and read on its front: "Space to let" and an arrow pointing upwards.

He motioned Saunders to join him and asked, "Where did this sign come from? It's light board, and it's been ripped down. Do you see anything to show where it was?"

"There, sarge," said Saunders, "on this side of the alley. The board tore and a corner is still up there. Which means the arrow should be pointing up … there."

"Any space to let is a possibility," said Doyle. "Call in our location, see if they have any other orders for us, and then follow me up this fire escape."

A minute later the two policemen were looking through a dirty window at an empty corridor. The door holding the window was stuck, but not locked. With sufficient effort they managed to force it open, and went in. The corridor was filthy, as if the last janitor had quit in disgust years ago. But there were marks in the dust and debris. Someone had been here recently.

Someone was still here. They heard a groan from up ahead. Moving quickly but alertly down the corridor, they found an open door and looked in. Lying on the floor, trying to raise herself up on an elbow, was Phyllis Radcliffe. She slipped and fell back, groaning again. Her clothes were torn and stained, her hair was completely disheveled, her lower lip was bloody and swollen, and her face was spotted with light bruises.

Doyle and Saunders rushed into the room and Doyle lifted her head. He noted the bruises, but felt no damage to the skull, or other bones.

"Call in for an ambulance, Dave," he told Saunders. "Then look for an elevator or some better way to get her down from here than that fire escape."

"How do you feel, Inspector? I'm Sergeant Frank Doyle. You met me the other day. You're safe now, and we've called for an ambulance. Do you need anything?"

"Water. Can you get me some water, please?" Phyllis croaked out. "I'm so thirsty. Call Paul, tell him I'm all right. Ow! Oh!   Just let me lie back on the floor and find me some water, please."

Down the hall was an empty soda bottle, and just beyond it, the washroom. Doyle picked up the bottle and brought it into the washroom. He was pleasantly surprised to find the water was still turned on. *Probably one water bill for the whole building,* he thought as he rinsed out the bottle several times. It still didn't look very clean, but it was all he had. He filled it up and brought it back to Phyllis.

She had managed to push herself up and was leaning back against the wall, looking like she had just lost the heavyweight championship. She took the bottle and drank a long drink. Doyle was going to warn her against drinking too much too fast, but she stopped herself. Another drink, and another, and then she said, "Where are we? And what time is it?"

"We're in a building just off Kenilworth on the south side of town," said Doyle, "and it's now about two-fifteen in the afternoon."

"The ambulance is on the way," said Saunders, coming in, "and there's an elevator at the end of the corridor. I checked it, and it works."

A siren, and another, and another announced the arrival of the ambulance and several police cars. Saunders ran back and took the elevator down to meet the ambulance men. Two stretcher bearers, a paramedic, and Paul Radcliffe returned with him. The medic checked Phyllis' bruises, felt her head for breaks or squishy places, and shown a light in her eyes to check her responsiveness.

Paul Radcliffe looked at his wife in shock and knelt down beside her. He knew she had been beaten, but seeing the reality of the beating made him angry.

"Darling, are you all right? Are you hurt badly?" he asked frantically.

"Hello, Paul," Phyllis said weakly. "I hurt all over, but I'll survive. Stay with me, I need a friendly face right now."

"You go with her, Inspector," said Doyle. "I don't think she's badly hurt. The bruises on her face are not that serious, but thugs usually don't stop at faces. They probably beat her in the body more. She'll need you, and you won't do us any good staying here and worrying about her. Forensics is on the way, too, and we can handle everything at this end."

"Thank you, Doyle," said Paul, sheepishly. "I'm supposed to be a tough cop, but that's my wife, and seeing her like….well, thanks for throwing me out. By the way, who found her?"

"Saunders and me," said Doyle, "we spotted a sign lying in the alley, and turned it over. It mentioned a space to let, and we went up, you know, just checking on empty spaces. We got lucky."

"So did my wife," said Paul. "Thanks for finding her. I'll see you both get a good recommendation for this. Helps at promotion time, you know."

The men lifted the stretcher and carried it down to the elevator, followed by the others. The elevator was small and there was barely room for the stretcher, the medics, and Paul Radcliffe.

"It was nice of him to offer us a recommendation," said Saunders, "but it was even nicer for you to share the credit with me for finding her. You were the one who spotted the sign."

"You are young, and you haven't been on the force all that long," said Doyle. "The guy that hogs all the credit may get promoted faster, but he makes no friends on the way up. The guy that shares the credit, even if he doesn't have to, makes friends, and they will help him make his way up, just the same. And they will keep helping him when he has gotten his promotion."

Chapter Thirteen

"I'd like to see Inspector Paul Radcliffe, please," said Sorenson to the new desk sergeant.

"Well, who wouldn't, he's a nice man," said the sergeant brusquely, "but he's also a busy man. He's a busy man almost every night, and tonight he is a very busy man. Good night."

"He asked me to stop by tonight," said Sorenson, calmly.

"Oh, he did, did he," said the sergeant rudely, "well, it must have slipped his mind, because he didn't put your name on the guest list. Beat it."

"It's about Mr. Roscoe Queen," said Sorenson, with just the right emphasis on the name.

"Oh, oh, well, why didn't you say so to begin with?" babbled the sergeant apologetically. "Room Four, on the right down this corridor."

Sorenson walked down the corridor glumly thinking, *It isn't what you know that gets results, it's who you know.*

***

The fried chicken is delicious, much tastier than I had expected, Sorenson thought. *No, come to think of it, Detective Mahoney had called it broasted chicken. Whatever it is, it is good and juicy. The biscuits are dry and heavy, though, and the rest of the fixings look dreadful. Well, at least the restaurant got the main item right.*

Mahoney had asked Sorenson to come back to the station for another conference. Paul Radcliffe was there, and Radcliffe's assistant Mike Feltz. Mahoney had already told him that Phyllis Radcliffe had been found, beaten up but alive and well. Sorenson was relieved to hear that. He was not responsible for her abduction, but he thought that she was a competent police officer. He liked competence, and he didn't like being on the bad side of the police. If she was safe, they would look a little more kindly at him.

"Help yourself to more chicken," said Mahoney, "we bought a ton of it because we might be here a long time. You don't have to stay all night, but we do want your point of view about some things. We're going to be here as long as it takes to find another clue."

"Phyllis will be joining us, too," said Paul. "I wanted her to rest at home after the hospital released her. But she wouldn't think of it. She wants to be in on the kill for this one. I can't say I blame her. I'm proud, too, to have so tough a wife."

"Thank you, Paul, for that unsolicited testimonial," laughed Phyllis as she came in. "Excuse my appearance, I can put makeup over the bruises but my lip is so sore I can't do lipstick. That's got to be worth another ten years on their sentences. And Paul, darling, even you are not going to see the rest of the bruises, not until they fade, anyway. Roscoe hits like a pile-driver, but he cut his hand on my belt buckle and gave the job to Leroy. Fortunately, Leroy pulled most of his punches so there's no internal damage. It still doesn't look nice.

"But I don't know that I would call it toughness. I didn't know what they wanted to know, and couldn't tell them anything, so they just kept beating me. Not talking was just ignorance, not toughness. Still, when we arrest them, give Leroy a little break. Roscoe told him to shoot me, and then left the room. Besides being light with his punches, Leroy shot the wall and followed him. That's worth something. Hand me some of that chicken, please."

They ate chicken and dry biscuits. A six-pack of drinkable beer appeared from a discreet brown bag, and helped wash down the biscuits. While they ate Mahoney filled everyone in on his morning's activities, ending with his interview with Ralph Stevens.

"So there we are," said Mahoney. "A rich foreigner now has these jewels, but we don't know who he is, or where he is, or what he might have done with them. That's why I wanted you here, Mr. Sorenson. You have a long streak now of lucky guesses, and we need another. And you have a unique perspective on people who are on the edge of the law. We can use that too."

"Mr. Sorenson?" asked Sorenson, "that's the first time you've called me that."

"I'm getting to like you, a little," said Mahoney, "and I noticed that you always refer to people as Mr., or Detective, or whatever. Very formal and polite. The only exception was Peterson. Why him?"

"Peterson and I were practically family," said Sorenson. "Mr. Inspector Radcliffe doesn't call his wife Mrs. Inspector Radcliffe. Formality isn't needed for family. I used to wait on big shots at good restaurants. That requires formality and courtesy. I am formal with others because it doesn't offend them. It may please them. And it costs me nothing. It's useful to not offend my clients, or thugs, or the police."

"Makes sense," said Mahoney, "now what can you tell us about rich foreigners? Do you know any in your line of work? Do you know any good places to find them?"

"I know some rich foreigners," said Sorenson, "but mostly Orientals. Chinese, some Japanese, people who worry about losing face. They like having a mistress, or making big bets, but they feel awkward actually making the payments. Paying a mistress is crass, beneath them, so I do it for them. There's a lot of other rich foreigners around, too, but they tend to be involved in things I won't touch. And some, like the Russians, have their own thugs to run errands.

"Looking for the Crown Jewels of Albania makes me think the Orientals are out of the picture. I know of a Chinese guy who wanted to steal a valuable jade collection a couple of years ago, but that was Chinese jade. I doubt he'd care about something Albanian."

"Really, who was this guy?" asked Feltz, sensing a chance for an arrest. "Did he actually steal it?"

"No," said Sorenson, "the jade belonged to a bigger, tougher Chinese fellow. I think the guy just managed to get back to China in one piece. I would look for a collector of European art or royal trophies. Maybe even the Albanian consulate – do they have a consulate in Chicago? It may even be someone from out of town who just happened to be here that day."

"Forget the consulate idea," said Mahoney. "I checked; they don't have a consulate here, the nearest one is in Detroit. It is possible the guy took the loot to the Albanian Embassy in DC, but I doubt it. The Albanians might have returned it, or, if they claimed it as a national treasure, it would have been in the news."

"Here's a picture of the loot," said Phyllis, "in case you haven't seen it yet.

"Yeah, the Star had this picture," said Sorenson.

"It's a nice enough crown and scepter and orb," said Phyllis, "but it's not spectacular. I don't know if it's actually worth the million that Stevens got, but it was worth that much to one person, anyway."

"The museum said it was worth probably half that," said Mahoney. "I checked with them this afternoon. It was nice stuff, but the craftsmanship was not first rate. And the crown is really just a fancy helmet, not a real crown. The jewels were worth a lot, and the thing is one of a kind and historic, but not so much as to be wildly valuable."

"So you're saying a collector wouldn't have paid that much for it," said Sorenson.

"Well, not an experienced collector," said Mahoney. "These guys will pay a bucket of money for something exotic or rare, but they don't like to waste their money either. If it takes a million to get something, they'll pay a million. But if they can get it for half a million, they can then afford to buy another one just like it."

"Thinking about it, now that you said that, I know just the type of guy," said Sorenson. "I know rich guys, and semi-rich guys, who like to show off. They want something impressive, and will pay anything to get it. One guy had me deliver $100,000 to a guy who was selling Elvis Presley's last jumpsuit on the sly. Elvis was too fat when he died to fit into that jumpsuit, but the buyer didn't think of that. All he cared about was the bragging rights. He had Elvis' last jumpsuit. He put it on display in his living room."

"So we're looking for a guy with money and an interest in Albanian crown jewels," said Phyllis. "That must make it a rich Albanian. How many rich Albanians are there in the greater Chicago area?"

"How many Albanians can there be here?" scoffed Feltz. "Do we celebrate Albanian New Year, or the feast day of the patron saint of Albania? Does Chicago dye the river on Albanian Independence Day?"

"Such a jerk you are," replied Mahoney. "Looking into this, I learned that John Belushi's parents were Albanian. He was a Chicago boy. So there. But, yeah, there's not a lot of them around."

"Well, that should make it easier to find a rich one," said Phyllis. "And remember, we have to find him before Roscoe finds out about him. And that reminds me, have you set a watch over Ralph Stevens? Or the other owners? Roscoe is going to try to find what happened to the jewels, too. He may not have our resources, but he's determined."

"They knew about Falkenberg," said Paul, "so they'll try to get to him first. And he's in Miami now, isn't he? That may make them think he took the jewels, sold them, and bought himself a new place a long way from here. So, Mike, get in touch with Miami PD and have them set up some protection for Mr. Falkenberg."

"Right away, boss," said Feltz, going into the outer office to find a list of police departments around the country.

"Sam, you should get some boys and cover the Hoovers and Rodriguez," said Paul.   "And Stevens. If Roscoe finds him, he'll get the worst treatment."

"I'll ask the Chicago cops to help with Stevens," said Mahoney. "They'd like to catch Roscoe, too, for a nice long list of crimes."

"The next step," said Phyllis, "is to do what Roscoe is going to do, in reverse. He's going to try to find the guy who took the loot, we've got to try to find Roscoe. Guarding these people is good, but it isn't always effective. It would be better for everyone if we found Roscoe before he can do any more damage. Any ideas where he might be, Mr. Sorenson?"

"They used to hang out at Biff Tollandson's bar," said Sorenson. "That was nine years ago, but they've been gone all this time. They might show up there again, from habit, maybe. It's worth checking out. You've got his old address on file, I suppose, but he'll be somewhere else now. Mr. Queen was never one of my favorite people, and I don't know too much about the places he liked. He did like to play the ponies, so you might try Hawthorne Park.

"But he's probably holed up somewhere, doing what you're doing, directing the search. If you have a list of his old haunts, try them, or places near them, or like them. Crooks and thugs are just as fond of a familiar and convivial spot as anyone else. Someplace shady, or at least with a disreputable reputation. But if he's lying low, trying not to show his face in town, then he'll just get a room and stay put.

"He had three guys looking for me, at least, and no one knew they worked for him. That means he's got a new gang. No surprise there. Mr. McGraw is dead, so that leaves Mr. Pasquale as the only other member of his gang that we know."

"You're slipping again, Mr. Sorenson," said Phyllis, "you forget that I've seen Cowboy, Leroy, and Hernando."

"No, I didn't forget them," said Sorenson, "but we don't know anything about them except for their names, and your description of their faces. We don't know where they came from, or if they have any connections here. Did Mr. Queen bring them with him? Probably, but from where? If Mr. Queen flew into Midway just the other night, one of these men had to have been here earlier to talk to Peterson. Maybe you can find where he was staying.

"The only sure thing is that Mr. Queen is going to keep them on a short leash. He never liked guys who failed him, and that must be why he had Mr. McGraw killed. He's not going to let the rest of his gang have a chance to fail him again. He'll keep them close by, where he can keep an eye on them. Even if he sends them out looking for the other buyers of the house, he'll expect them to return regularly. And they'll stay wherever he stays.

"There is one thing you can do to flush him out. Has the department made any announcement about your rescue?"

"Not yet," said Paul, "I'm still trying to decide how to play that. Should we keep the pressure on as if we were still searching for her?"

"No," said Sorenson, "increase the pressure. Issue a statement that she's been found dead. Offer a reward, if the city will let you. Anyone who is hiding him or letting him hang out, is going to be afraid of being an accomplice. He's going to have fewer places to go safely, fewer friends willing to help him. Keep his picture and the others on the TV news, and online. The drawings from Mrs. Inspector Radcliffe's descriptions can be passed off as from eyewitnesses to the kidnapping. Keep the heat on."

Chapter Fourteen

The tavern had been closed down by the city for selling alcohol to minors. The most recent was a teen driver who had left the bar late one night under the influence of several stiff whiskeys, and the delusion that he was at the Indianapolis Speedway. Fortunately, no one was hurt in his mad dash through town, or in his only-to-be-expected crash. His car, worth rather little before his drive, was now worth absolutely nothing. He was too drunk to tell the police his name, much less where he had gotten drunk. But the next morning, stiff, sore, mostly sober, and very scared, he was more than willing to name the bar. He was the fourth under-age patron of a generous but stupid bar owner, and the city of Berwyn did not see any reason to wait for a fifth.

But that was just the top of the list, the most serious reason to close the bar. The Health Department had been in the bar two days before the teen had driven off to disaster. Their report added several other reasons to close the bar. Rats, mice, cockroaches, and other types of pests ran freely around the basement, and visited the bar area frequently. Exterminators had worked for two days to eliminate them, but the vermin had returned to the empty tavern.

The place stunk. There was a lingering odor of urine, mixed with some other, worse, smell. Cleaning seemed to have no effect on the smells. The landlord had tried three different professional cleaning companies, but to no avail. He had almost given up hope of unloading the property at any price.

The roof leaked badly when it rained hard, and dripped when it rained a little. A hasty coat of tar on the flat roof had helped a bit, but did not entirely keep the rain out. The walls were cracked in places, and it was not all just cracks in the plaster. The larger cracks were in the brickwork of the building, as the Building Inspector noted.

Almost nothing about the building was desirable, which made it an almost perfect hide-out for Roscoe Queen and his men. Leroy had jimmied the back door and they had settled in. Louie had found a bucket of left-over tar and a brush and told Cowboy to paint over the front windows. A store next door down the alley had an outside electrical outlet, and they used a long extension cord to tap it for their own lights. The blackened windows would keep the lights from being seen outside.

They were used to bad smelling dives, and a certain amount of vermin, but this was a prize winner. None of them liked the smell, or the aggressive roaches. The rats and mice were a little less intrusive, but only when the men were awake. Once they went to sleep, they could feel things crawling all over them.

Roscoe Queen was unhappy. The police search for the missing cop had brought too much publicity his way, and it had forced him to leave Biff Tollandson's bar. Biff himself had dared to "ask" him to leave, like he was no longer welcome there. And his gang hadn't found out anything about the buyers of the house, despite spending all day on it. He didn't like waiting. He didn't like not getting results. He was very unhappy.

"Roscoe, I know you're upset," said Louie. "You're upset about Biff tossing you out on the street, but it's been a long time since you done him any favors. You're upset about this dump, but we're lucky to have any hideout at all. You're upset because the guys haven't found out who has the loot. Give them a little time. This ain't what we normally do.

"And the main problem is that the cops are looking for you real hard. I agree we had to talk to that female cop, but I told you kidnapping her was a bad idea. Now we've got the whole police force out looking for her, and us."

"Yeah, you told me it was a bad idea," said Roscoe, "but you didn't offer me a better one. 'Send Leroy around to ask about damage to the fireplace' – she wouldn't have been fooled by that line. Honestly, Louie, was that the best you could come up with? It's not like any of us look respectable or business-like. Even if she had the stuff, she wouldn't just turn it over because we asked for it, pretty please."

"It's only going to get worse when they find her body," said Louie. "All hell will break loose then. You know as well as I do that there's nothing that a cop hates more than a cop killer. They won't rest until they find us. So we just have to lay low until we get the jewels and then we can skip out. We don't need to sell them here. We might get a better price in New York, anyway."

"Yeah, yeah," said Roscoe, "OK, just go ahead and say I screwed up. Louie, you're the only man I'll let talk to me this way. Maybe I shouldn't have kidnapped the cop. But how else was I going to find out she didn't have the stuff. And if I hadn't killed her, she could have identified us all. How was I to know the cops already knew it was us that grabbed her? I know we got to hide, but really, this place is terrible. I'm afraid the ceiling is going to fall in on us."

"Yeah, this place is a dump," said Louie, "but a condemned building is a good hideout. And that's what we need right now. It is so run down the cops won't bother looking here. And we managed to get in without tearing down the boards blocking the door, and the back door still looks locked. So it looks unoccupied. Even with a big man-hunt on, we can hide here for a couple of weeks if we have to. There's a burger joint and a liquor store just down the street, and Hernando can blend in with the Hispanics around here and get us food and drink."

The loud noise of something falling over, followed by a long stream of profanity, announced the arrival of Cowboy and Leroy.

"Goddamn step!" yelled Cowboy angrily, "who'd put a two-inch step goin' up into a back door? That's the third time I've tripped over it. Couldn't we have found a better hideout?"

"Quit your beefing, Cowboy," said Louie, "and try to remember the step next time you come in. It's not going anywhere. What have you got for us?"

"Oh, hell, I ain't got nothin' for you at all, Roscoe," said Cowboy. "I couldn't get anywhere with those real estate people. They kept tryin' to sell me some other house. Didn't understand what I was tryin' to ask."

"I got something for you, boss," said Leroy. "I've got the address of that Falkenberg guy, and the guy who bought the house from him."

"Well, finally," said Roscoe, "about time you guys started getting some results. Okay, where does this guy live now?"

"Miami, boss," said Leroy, "here's the address I got from the real estate gal. And here's the guy who bought it from Falkenberg, a guy named Hoover. He's still in the area, got a business here."

"So Falkenberg sold to Hoover, and Hoover sold to the cops," said Louie. "That should make it easier to find out who took the stuff."

"No," said Leroy, "Hoover wasn't the one who sold to the cops. He sold to some guy named Rodriguez. He defaulted on his loan, and embezzled some money, and went to jail. The cops bought the house from his bank."

"So if Rodriguez is in jail, we ain't going to be able to talk to him," said Roscoe.

"No, he ain't in jail anymore," said Leroy. "I met a guy who knows a guy whose brother is a guard at the jail. The guard says Rodriguez got out a couple of months ago."

"Don't matter," said Louie, "he can't be the guy. If he defaulted on his mortgage, and he embezzled from his boss, he didn't have any money. Which means he didn't sell the jewels. Which means he didn't take the jewels. So, it's got to be Falkenberg, or Hoover."

"And Falkenberg moved to Miami," said Roscoe. "That sounds like a step up in society – Berwyn to Miami. The kind of thing a guy who just came into a lot of money might do. Let's go pay Mr. Falkenberg a little visit. We need to get out of town anyway, before the cops find the dead cop, and really start hunting for us."

"Hernando," said Louie, "there's a used car dealer down the street. Go down and steal us a nice comfy looking van. Leroy, you steal a different license plate for the van. Cowboy, get us a bag of burgers and some beer. We're going to be in for a long drive."

"How long is it going to take to get to Miami?" asked Roscoe.

"We drove down in 2003 for the World Series, remember?" said Louie. "It took 21 hours each way, total. We weren't in a hurry then, and we spent three days going down there. That was just the two of us driving. We've got five drivers now, and I don't think you want to waste any time.

"Let me work this out. Gimme a minute. Ah, yeah, if we each drive for four hours, we can do it in about a day. We'll have to stop for gas and to hit the can, and we can stretch our legs when we do. If we leave now, say nine o'clock, we can be in Miami this time tomorrow night. We can get a place to crash overnight, and go see Falkenberg in the morning."

"We can see him tomorrow night just as easily," said Roscoe. "Guys are more agreeable when they haven't had a good night's sleep. And I'm more irritable when I haven't had a good night's sleep. And the sooner we get the loot, the better I'm going to like it."

"You're the boss, Roscoe," said Louie. "I don't want to waste time, either."

***

"I got a big Grand Caravan, boss," said Hernando. "It seats seven, so we can use the big back seat as a bed. It'll be a little cramped, and the rest of us will have to sleep sitting up, but that's OK. Give me a minute to take the plates off. As soon as Leroy brings me another set, we can go."

"Toss those old plates in the bar," said Louie, "we don't want the cops finding them too soon. If they find them, they'll know we switched them."

"Good choice, Hernando," said Roscoe, out in the alley. "I like the silver color. I see a lot of these on the streets, so it won't stand out."

"Thanks, boss," said Hernando, "but it's just luck. This was the only big van they had on the lot."

"I found a nice set of really muddy plates," said Leroy, coming up. "These will be hard to read unless you're standing next to them. Make it harder for cops to show an interest in us."

"Where the hell's Cowboy?" grumbled Roscoe. "I don't want to have to stop to get food later. What's keeping him, anyway? Two stops he had to make, and they're both just down the street."

"Here he comes, boss," said Louie, "and there's why he's so slow."

Cowboy came slowly up the alley, struggling with a large bag of burgers in one hand, and a case of beer barely held under his other arm. The beer kept trying to slip from his grasp, and he was constantly jerking it higher on his hip. With a little help from Leroy, the food and beer were loaded into the van.

***

They didn't have a map, so Louie's memory of the trip to the World Series had to serve instead. Louie drove first, since he had a better sense of direction and the route than Roscoe, and the other three had never lived around Chicago. He went west to Harlem, then turned south to the Stevenson.

He was a city boy all the way, but he liked driving on the expressways. City boy or not, as a life-long criminal, he never took public transportation. He believed there was a reason it was called a get-away *car*. But even fleeing a crime scene, there was too much traffic to deal with in a city. He just couldn't really open up and fly. But on an expressway, he could go almost as fast as he wanted, and there were no stoplights.

For this trip, speed was important. The faster they drove, the sooner they would be in Miami. But if speed was good, it was also dangerous. Louie wasn't worried about a crash, they were all good at driving cars. But attracting the attention of a state trooper would be a disaster. So Louie instructed the others in how to use the cruise control in the van, and then set it for just above the speed limit. Cops always gave a little slack about fast driving as long as you weren't reckless. Maximum speed, minimum notice.

Louie then had Hernando write down the list of cities they would be going through as he recited them. He told them to look for the highway signs that would lead them to the next city, and they couldn't get lost. He hoped he was right about that. Maybe they could find a map when they stopped for gas.

Roscoe had a burger and a beer with the others, and they set up their shifts for driving. Louie would drive first, taking them out of the Chicago area confusion of interstates, and Roscoe would take the next shift. He would nap in one of the second row seats first, and let Cowboy have the bed-like back seat. Cowboy, presumably well rested, would take over from Roscoe, and Roscoe would take the bed. Leroy and Hernando would share the last two legs.

They also discussed their plans for handling Falkenberg. Louie, who looked the least disreputable of them, would approach Falkenberg.

"I figure the cops know as much as we do, Roscoe," said Louie. "Maybe more, so they have probably talked to Falkenberg. But if he's got the loot, I think he won't have had time to turn it in to anybody. So, I can pretend I'm a reporter working on a story about the stolen jewels, which we just learned about. I can ask him all kinds of questions and he'll just think it's for the story.

"If he has the stuff, we grab it from him. If he never had it, we come back to Berwyn. And if he had it and gave it to the Florida cops already, we find a way to steal it from them. And if he sold it, which I really think he did, we find out who he sold it to. And we go looking for that guy."

"That's a good plan, Louie," said Roscoe, "it covers all the angles pretty well."

***

Hernando had been doubly lucky in stealing this van. It was not only spacious enough for them, it had almost half a tank of gas. They had refueled in Indiana, but found only Indiana and Illinois maps. As dawn was breaking near Chattanooga, Cowboy had to pull into another gas station. By this time, Louie had forgotten about wanting a map. They were halfway to Miami and hadn't gotten lost yet.

Roscoe was still sleeping soundly on the back seat, and no one wanted to risk angering him by waking him up just because they had stopped for gas. While Hernando filled the tank, the others got out to get a little circulation back into their cramped legs. Cowboy got himself an extra large coffee and a couple of doughnuts to help keep him awake for the rest of his shift. Leroy got some licorice for himself and Hernando's favorite, some beef jerky. Louie, making sure nothing went wrong inside and that everyone was back in the van, paid the cashier for the gas, and joined the others. He went back to sleep as Cowboy got back on the expressway.

***

Cowboy drove on through Atlanta to Macon, Georgia before giving up the wheel. Leroy took over and pushed on to Orlando, Florida before he got too tired to drive. Louie's estimate of the time had been a bit off, and Cowboy and Leroy had taken longer shifts than they were supposed to. This left Hernando with only the last four hours to drive. The sun was getting low in the sky, and the highway traffic dwindled down to a bunch of semis heading for Miami, same as them.

Roscoe was getting fidgety, something that Louie did not like to see. The seats did not feel as comfortable now as they had when they started out. He knew that an uncomfortable Roscoe was an irritated Roscoe, and that an irritated Roscoe might do something rash. Louie knew he couldn't do anything about Roscoe's comfort, so he tried to distract him.

"What do you think the jewels are worth, Roscoe?" Louie asked. "When we took them, you thought they'd bring half a million. Do you think they might be worth more now?"

"They can't be worth any less," said Roscoe, his mind diverted from the lumpy seat. "Jewels never lose value. Whether they've gone up is hard to say. These were jewels from some nickel and dime country in Europe. I never even heard of it before. If it was the French crown jewels, or the German crown jewels, private collectors would pay through the nose for them. But for these, I don't know. Still, jewels is jewels. There's always a market for high end jewels."

"Say, Roscoe," said Leroy, hesitantly, "you ain't never told us what our shares in this thing were going to be. You said it wouldn't be our normal split, but you didn't say what it would be. I ain't complaining, mind you. I know you'll do all right by us. I would just, you know, like to know how much I'm going to get."

"I've been thinking about that," said Roscoe. "I was going to break it out like this, each of us gets one share, then Louie and I get an extra share for stealing the loot, then I get an extra share for being the boss. That's eight shares, so you'd get one eighth of the payout. So if it's worth $500,000, you would get a bit more than sixty grand.

"But I want to do more for you, so I'm going to give you three guys a hundred grand each, and Louie and I will take the rest. If we can get more for the loot, you'll get a bigger share. Fair enough?"

"That sounds pretty good, boss," said Leroy, along with the others.

And when did Roscoe ever take the small piece of a pie? Louie thought to himself. *He won't give me the shaft, he needs me too much, and he knows it. I wonder what game he's playing. Does he think it's worth more now? The boys won't know what he actually sells the stuff for, so he really doesn't have to give them a bigger share.*

Or is he planning to get rid of some of the boys? We've already lost Whitey and Joe. He needs a gang. He's always had a gang, and he doesn't know how to operate without one. It was hard enough when we left Berwyn after the bank job disaster, when we lost almost the whole gang. These aren't the best guys I've ever worked with, but they ain't all that bad. If he dumps them, where does he think he's going to find more guys?

"Hey, Louie," said Hernando from the driver's seat, "we're in Miami now. Where is this guy's place? And are we going there tonight or in the morning? Should I look for a motel, or what?"

"It's getting toward evening," said Louie. "By the time we find his place, it'll be after 6, maybe 7. But that's not too late for the reporter gag. What do you think, Roscoe? Wanna go there now?"

"Yeah, I think so," said Roscoe. "At least, if you feel up to pulling this guy's leg with your song and dance. But whatever he tells us, we're going to need a motel afterward. I want a real bed tonight."

Chapter Fifteen

Falkenberg lived in the Coconut Grove neighborhood of Miami, and Louie was impressed by the very nice houses they drove past. Large, sprawling houses with big, green lawns, but hardly any palm trees. A place called Coconut Grove with no palm trees just didn't seem right. No sidewalks, either, no curbs and gutters, no one out walking a dog, no one out walking at all. It was a far cry from Berwyn.

"I hope he hasn't put all the money into his house," said Roscoe, grumpily. "These places look a lot more expensive than that house in Berwyn. If he put the cash into a house, we'll never get it. You've got to pump him carefully, Louie, make sure you get everything out of him."

"Don't worry, Roscoe," said Louie, "I can sweet-talk a kid into giving me his ice cream cone. Besides, if he sold the stuff, we just need to find out who he sold it to. This should be easy as pie. We're getting close now, Hernando, yeah, there it is, on the right. Pull over and wait. It shouldn't take more than half an hour."

Louie stepped out of the van and strolled up the walk to the front door. A casually dressed man in a car parked in a driveway across the street sorted through a set of small photographs lying on the passenger seat and soon found a picture of Louie. He called his office at the Miami Police department, and asked for backup. Then he turned on a small camera on his dash which fed a series of pictures to a laptop.

Louie knocked on the door, and looked around at the garden in front of the house while waiting for someone to answer his knock. He looked at the large tree in the middle of the lawn. He looked at a tabby cat slinking across the lawn. He waited some more. Louie was about to leave when the door opened, and a man in late middle age appeared.

"May I help you?" asked the man. "Are you looking for someone?"

"Ah, yes," said Louie, "are you Mr. Arthur Falkenberg, formerly of Berwyn, Illinois?"

"Yes, I am," said Falkenberg, "what do you want?"

"My name is Peter Winkler, and I'm a reporter for the Miami Herald," said Louie. "We just found out about a mysterious case back in Berwyn, involving a house you used to own. The Berwyn press is reporting that some valuable jewels had been hidden in that house.

Recently the house was vandalized and the jewels were stolen. Your name
was mentioned as a former owner of the house, so, since you live here
now, we would like to interview you. You know, local angle on an
unusual case. May I come in and talk to you?"

Two more unmarked squads came rolling slowly down the street,
one from each end of the street. One stopped by the driveway with the
first car, partly blocking the street. The other pulled up behind the van,
but near the center of the street. In the distance, sirens wailed in the
twilight, coming closer.

Louie, hearing the sirens, looked around at the street and saw two
cars parked in a suspicious manner near the van. Cursing, he ran back to
the van as Roscoe opened the side door. Louie jumped in and Hernando
gunned the engine, pulling hard on the steering wheel. The van spun
around, ran over the grass on the other side of the street, and just missed
hitting the car behind it.

"Damn cops were waiting for us," said Louie. "Falkenberg stalled
answering the door, and they must have had somebody watching the place.
If he still has the jewels, the police will take them now. Damn! And I
was just about to go in with him."

"Good thing you didn't," said Roscoe. "We'd have had to leave you
or we'd all have been picked up. How the hell did they know it was you?"

"Cops talk to each other, all over the country," said Leroy. "If the
Berwyn cops knew it was us, then every other cop in the country will
know."

Hernando was driving as fast as the van could go without crashing
into other cars, weaving around them as much as he could. Behind them,
three unmarked cars with flashing blue lights on their dashboards and two
squad cars were closing in.

"Turn right at the next corner," said Louie, spotting a highway sign
ahead. "Get on the Dixie Highway and that will lead us to the interstate.
Maybe we can lose them there."

The light was red, but Hernando didn't slow down. The van
careened around the corner heading east, barely staying in contact with the
pavement. An eastbound bus driver, entering the intersection just behind
them, slammed on his brakes and skidded his bus to a stop. He blocked
the eastbound lanes, and hit a west bound car, stopping the rest of the

traffic with the accident. Roscoe looked out the rear window of the van and saw their pursuers trying vainly to work their way through the jammed up vehicles.

"Forget the interstate," said Roscoe, "we're losing them now. They'll expect us to take that and they'll have cops lining the highway for miles. Get off of this road as soon as you can, and we'll look for a place to hole up for the night. A small motel will do. The cops may have our pictures, but the motels won't. And slow down, we don't want to attract any more attention."

Hernando pulled off the highway and cruised slowly through the evening. He spotted a small, unimpressive motel and started to pull into its lot.

"Not this one," said Roscoe. "I want a good night's sleep, and a dive like this is going to have lumpy mattresses. Up the road there, see that sign, Best Western. That'll do nicely. I've got a fake credit card I've been hanging on to for just this emergency. Leroy, when we get into our rooms, come back out and dump this van someplace.

"Don't worry about wiping it down. The cops know we stole it, and it will take them some time to get our fingerprints. Take the license plates off and dump them somewhere. Tomorrow I want you to find us another van, if you can."

***

It was eight-thirty before they settled in and came down to eat. The hotel restaurant was no longer crowded and the gang was able to get a table in a corner booth away from the few remaining diners. Roscoe took the innermost seat so he could watch the entire room. He shifted his gun to the waistband of his slacks to make it easier to grab. He didn't think the cops could find them here, but he was taking no chances.

They didn't talk while the waiter took their orders. They would pretend to be just five friends out for a late dinner. If they didn't say anything suspicious in front of the staff, no one would call the police. They had tired of the burgers quickly, and then those ran out. It had been a long, tiring day, ending in frustration over their plan misfiring. So they ordered the best items on the menu. Since the meal was going to be charged to the same fake credit card as their rooms, they ate well and expensively.

"Your plan didn't work, Louie," said Roscoe with a very quiet voice. "What are we going to do now? We can't go back and talk to Falkenberg. And if he has the loot and gives it to the police now, they'll be watching it so hard that we won't have a chance to steal it from them."

"We still got options here, Roscoe," said Louie, wary of Roscoe's tone of voice. "I think they'll tell us what we want to know tomorrow. That accident with the bus will get in the news, and the news guys will find out about the chase. And they'll find out about Falkenberg, and why he's so important. And then they will tell us whether he ever had the jewels, or not. And if he did, they will tell us what he did with them. News guys love to tell everything they know about anything.

"We just need to watch the late night news, and the morning news, and grab a newspaper in the morning. The story will be there, we find out what we need to know, and we go on from there. I think he sold the jewels, and the story will tell us who bought them. And that's our next stop."

"And what if the cops are waiting there, too?" asked Roscoe. "What do we do then?"

"We don't approach the next guy the same way," said Louie. "We will know he has the jewels. He bought them so he could keep them for himself. We case his house, looking for the cops. We avoid them, or knock them out and tie them up. We get around them somehow. The rest is just an easy burglary then."

"Okay, Louie," said Roscoe, "it sounds like it'll work. But what if Falkenberg never had the jewels in the first place?"

"We have Hoover and Rodriguez to check out back in Berwyn. I don't think it's Rodriguez, because of his money problems. That means it's Hoover. He's got a business, so we can grab him going to or from his business, and squeeze it out of him."

"The cops will be watching him, too," said Roscoe. "They're probably watching everybody who's got any connection to the loot, even guys we don't know about."

"Yeah, but they aren't going to have an army watching him," said Louie. "Berwyn's not Chicago or Miami, it don't have nearly as many cops. My mistake with Falkenberg was that I didn't expect the cops to be watching him. If we had gone in the back way, the cop out front wouldn't have seen anything, and we'd have been fine.

"With Hoover, they'll have one cop watching him, so we get one guy to decoy the cop out of the way. Then we can grab Hoover without any trouble. We may not even have to sucker the cop if we can grab Hoover fast enough. A cop in front of his business can't follow out the back door. If he does, somehow, he's on foot and we're in a car, speeding away."

"Okay, Louie," said Cowboy uncertainly, "we can grab this guy, or that guy, or anybody. But do any of these guys still have the loot? You said it was a crown and a bunch of other royal gear. Who's goin' to keep this kind of stuff? If I found this crap, I'd sell it as fast as I could. I can use money, I can't use a crown. So if the guy sold the jewels, who bought them? Isn't that the guy we should be lookin' for?"

"You're right, Cowboy," said Roscoe, "but we don't know that guy's name. We have to squeeze it out of the guy that found the jewels. He's the only guy who knows who bought the stuff. If Falkenberg didn't have the jewels, we go after Hoover.   If Falkenberg did have the jewels, and sold them, the news will tell us who bought them and we go after that guy. A bit more discreetly this time."

***

They had rented three rooms, all very standard motel rooms. A pair of large beds, a long counter that served as a dresser and a surface to place things on, and a TV.   There were two beds in each room, and five men, none of whom wanted to share a bed with any of the others. It would have been extravagant, but with a fake credit card the cost was immaterial. And it gave them three televisions to watch the nightly news.

It turned out that all the stations had attended the same single press briefing, so they all told variations on the same story. They all showed the traffic accident and the crashed bus. They all showed a police captain talking about the dangerous criminals who were being sought. They all talked about how the criminals had already kidnapped and killed a policewoman in Berwyn, and how they had undoubtedly tried to kidnap

Mr. Falkenberg. But only station WSVN had an exclusive interview with
Falkenberg.

"The Berwyn police had contacted me twice about this case," said
Mr. Falkenberg, basking in his new fame. "And the Miami police were
cooperating with them to give me protection. I did my part by keeping the
kidnapper busy until the police arrived."

Here he skipped over the less glamorous part about being in the
bathroom when he first heard the knock on his door.

"The police had warned me to be careful of any strangers showing
up at my door, but I had every confidence that they would protect me.
And they came very quickly when the thug knocked on my door. "

"Why were these criminals trying to kidnap you, Mr. Falkenberg?"
asked the reporter.

"The Berwyn police said it was about the Albanian Crown Jewels,"
replied Falkenberg. "They had apparently been hidden in a house I once
owned in Berwyn, a nice house, too. The house is now owned by the
policewoman who was killed. They ransacked it, obviously looking for
the jewels, and didn't find them. I guess the thugs thought I had found
them when I owned the house. I never imagined there could be a treasure
hidden in the house, of course."

"Well, Louie," said Roscoe, entering Louie's room, "Falkenberg
didn't have them after all. We've wasted a lot of time coming down here,
and almost got caught into the bargain.   Tell the boys that we'll go back
tomorrow, but we'll do it in two days. The trip down here almost killed
me."

***

"I got the Chrysler version of that Grand Caravan we had, boss" said
Hernando. "It's got more comfortable seats, which I knew you wanted.
And Leroy snagged some Georgia license plates, so the cops won't notice
us so much. The dealer I took the van from doesn't open until noon on
Sunday, so we've got a couple of hours before it's going to be missed."

"Hey, Roscoe, Hernando did real good," said Louie. "This baby has
GPS, we can ask it for directions."

"So what?" replied Roscoe. "You know the way. It's the same both ways, we go back the way we came."

"Nah, we're hot now," said Louie. "They're going to expect us to go back to Berwyn, and they'll be watching the shortest route, which is how we came down. I got a good map from the desk clerk and I found a more roundabout way home."

"Roundabout just means it'll take more time," complained Roscoe. "I don't want to waste time getting back to Berwyn. Every day we spend without getting those jewels is a day we can't disappear from the cops' radar."

"I know you don't want to waste time," said Louie, "but the dealer is going to report this van stolen in a few hours. And the cops will be looking at all copper colored Chrysler vans on the interstate. They ain't going to be worried about what state's tags are on it, either. If we take a slightly, and I emphasize slightly, longer route home, we'll miss a lot of those cops. And not running into cops is going to make a shorter and safer trip home."

"Okay, Louie, you work it out," said Roscoe, "but try to keep it around two days total. I already said we could take an extra day. I don't want any more if you can avoid it."

"Look, we can go by way of Tallahassee, cutting over to the west side of the state first. Then across to Jackson, Mississippi, up to St. Louis, and then home to Berwyn. None of the same highways, nothing directly north to Chicago until the last leg, nothing obvious."

Chapter Sixteen

Zef Tanush turned on his computer and did what he always did, first thing every morning. He looked for news about Albania. He was glad he had left Albania, mainly because he had been poor there, and he was rich in America. Life had been hard there, but once the Communist government fell, things started to get better. He had made a bit of money, not a lot, but enough to leave for America. But he still felt proud to be an Albanian. It was why he had bought the incredibly beautiful crown resting on the shelf to his right.

Even though he no longer cared about the politics of his homeland, he cared about its people, culture, and history. He was always curious about what was happening back home. Was there a new artist or musician or playwright who needed support? He had the money to help them out, and he enjoyed helping them. He felt he was helping create a new, improved Albania, using his money and their talents. He was like those Italian dukes in the Renaissance, paying artists to make beauty.

And today's news was…. Albanian Crown Jewels! *Oh my god*, he thought. *There are thieves and murderers looking to steal my treasures. Oh, my, they kidnapped and killed a policewoman! They tried to kidnap this man in Florida – will they try to kidnap me, too? What will happen to me? What will happen to Ajola?*

Wait. Wait. How can they find me? I bought the jewels from some American. I don't know his name. He doesn't know my name. He doesn't know where I live. Even if the criminals could find him, he can't tell them who I am or where I live. I'm safe. Ajola is safe, which is more important.

Oh, but wait again. I'm a rich Albanian-American. The Crown Jewels are Albanian. The thieves may think that a rich Albanian may have bought them. And I am known to be a rich Albanian-American. Well-known. My name can be found easily, and my address.

I must hide the jewels. Tomorrow I must go to the bank and put them in my safe deposit box. It is a big box. Will it all fit into that box? I hope so. And I must take Ajola away from the danger here. Perhaps we could take a vacation. Maybe back to visit our families in Tirana. It's been two years since we went back last time.

A month with our relatives will be pleasant and safer than staying here. Zamir can tell us when it is safe to come back. Yes, that is what we must do.

***

Ralph Stevens wasn't interested in international news, or the culture of exotic foreign lands. He was only interested in how his stocks were doing, and how close the Cubs were to clinching their division again. Thenews.com gave him both on one page. He could customize it to give him just the news he wanted, with a smattering of big headlines about other news.

He logged in and glanced at his stocks. He had checked them yesterday, no need to look again on a Sunday. The Cubs were doing well, winning the first two games against St. Louis. One last game today to decide the division winner. He wished he had bought tickets, but it was too late now. The last home stand had been sold out for weeks. What other news was there?

"Albanian Crown Jewels Thriller – Car Chase – Kidnap Attempt"

Ralph turned pale, and slumped in his chair as he read the story and saw the picture. *Oh, no,* he thought, *serious criminals are after those jewels. If the cops could find me so could these thugs. The police have a man watching the house, but is one man enough? What if the crooks come in the back way? And will the cops give me really good protection, or use me as bait to catch the thieves?*

If the thugs find me like the police did, they'll try to make me tell them who I sold the jewels to. And they aren't likely to believe I don't know. What would they do to me? I don't even want to think about that. If they killed a female cop, they aren't going to be nice to me.

Alice and I should go somewhere for a few days. Tell the cops we're leaving, but not where we're going to go. The cops could call us when it's safe to come home. It's almost October, maybe we could go to Vermont and look at the fall foliage. Alice likes that sort of thing. And it will be far away and safe. No one will think I'll be there.

***

"Good morning, Mr. Sorenson," said Phyllis Radcliffe. "How are you this bright, sunny morning?"

"I'm awake," he replied, "I've had my breakfast, and I've been wondering if Mr. Queen's thugs sleep in on a Sunday morning. I'd like to go out and get a newspaper, if it's not too dangerous. And what are you doing calling me? Don't they ever let you have a day off?"

"Technically, yesterday and today are my days off, this week," said Phyllis. "But only because I'm supposed to be dead. Hot cases get worked hard. Days off are for wimps. I'm not a wimp."

"I never thought you were," said Sorenson, "and Friday showed proof that you weren't. I've been beaten by some tough guys in my time, and they mostly pound the body. It hurts a little, then a lot, then a lot more. And you show up for Paul's council of war just hours later. I've known men who couldn't do that."

"Thanks for the compliment," said Phyllis. "I wasn't fishing for one. I don't need to, everyone is saying how tough I am. It wasn't too terrible, because Leroy pulled his punches. Still, I ache all over and, well, if you've been beaten by thugs, I don't have to describe it to you. It's not fun, and it's not much of an honor to take it and get back up. But it is a dishonor, a personal dishonor, to wimp out.

"Enough talk about how tough I am. I've got some good news for your plans for today. Roscoe and friends have gone to Florida to look for Falkenberg. It looks like he took all of his boys with him, so you should be safe on the street today.

"Miami police think he was trying to kidnap Falkenberg. At least, Roscoe would have wanted to ask him about the fireplace and the jewels. Anyway, the cops were watching and the backup arrived in force before Roscoe or his boys could do anything. There was a chase, but Roscoe got away.

"The Miami news gave out the report that Falkenberg never had the jewels. Roscoe was likely listening to the news to see what the Miami police were doing to find him. So, if he was paying attention, he knows now that he wasted his time going south. He's probably coming back here to look for Hoover. If he wasn't listening to the news, he's still in Miami trying to find another way to get to Falkenberg.

"We figure Roscoe left after ordering my death, and took two days to go south. Two more days coming back means he'll be here late Monday or early Tuesday. Or a day later if he's still going for Falkenberg. We're going to put Mr. Hoover and his wife up in a hotel for the next few days. We don't have to worry about the bricklayer if Hoover isn't around to give up his name."

"Well, it's nice to know that I can go for a walk, Inspector," said Sorenson. "But I only need to go a few doors down the street for my newspaper. I guess you would like me to take a longer walk."

"Yeah, I threw in the casual talk so it wouldn't sound like an order," said Phyllis. "But Paul and Mahoney are in the office now, and would like to pick your brains some more. Any time you show up will be fine. They're working on leads to rich Albanians, and would like your opinion."

"Certainly, it beats sitting around here avoiding gangsters by staying invisible," said Sorenson. "Tell them I'll be there in half an hour."

***

On Sundays the buses ran on a reduced schedule, which Sorenson forgot, and he had to wait fifteen minutes because the eleven o'clock weekday bus was an eleven-fifteen Sunday bus. He decided that he could be a little less careful today with all the thugs out of town, especially since his destination was the police station. So he skipped two changes of bus, and got to the station house almost at his half hour estimate.

"I told you already I don't know any rich Albanians," Sorenson said as he entered Paul's office. "No, to be exact, I don't know any rich people whom I know to be Albanian. It's possible that some rich Albanian has changed his name to something more American. Lots of people do that, just to blend in. And I may know a rich guy is foreign, without knowing what brand of foreign he is.

"Albania is in the Balkans, along with Serbia, Montenegro, and a bunch of other dinky countries. I'd know a Greek on sight, most likely, but not any of the others. I'd recognize someone speaking Greek, too, because I used to hang out in Greektown once upon a time. But all the other languages and accents wouldn't mean a thing to me. I also wouldn't know an Albanian name if I saw or heard one. So it's possible that I do know a rich Albanian, and don't know that I know one."

"Fair enough, Mr. Sorenson," said Mahoney, "I've given up on thinking you're holding out on us. Not with your life on the line. That last remark you made is why we wanted to talk to you again. Maybe you know some guys and don't know their ethnic background. Maybe they're hiding it, maybe they never told you, maybe you never asked.

"We've got a list of people in the Chicago area who came from Albania. There's only a few thousand Albanians in and around Chicago, mostly in the outer suburbs. It's not a terribly long list and we've already thrown out the ones who aren't worth at least a million. That makes for a much shorter list, and we would like to go over it with you. We want you to think about each name, and tell us if it rings any bells."

There were a dozen names on the list, and Sorenson did not recognize any of them. He did not even have to hesitate about any of the names. They were all unfamiliar to him.

"I never heard of any of these guys," said Sorenson. "They're either too honest to need my services, or they have their own errand boys. Where did you get this list of names, anyway?"

"The Census Bureau in DC will do favors if we ask nicely," said Paul, "and we asked really nicely. They gave us the list of all Chicago area residents of Albanian ethnic origin. This is as good as it gets."

"And yet," mused Sorenson, "and yet, it may not be complete. The last census was eight years ago, and people move. Suppose our rich Albanian was living in New York, or Detroit, where they have a consulate. The census was in 2010, and the jewels were found and sold in 2013. That's a three year window for him to move to Chicago, or nearby. Which is why he is not on your list."

"He's doing it again, Paul," complained Mahoney, "he's pulling good answers right out of the air. How do you do this, Mr. Sorenson? I've got two assistants that could learn a lot from you if you can teach how you do this."

"You're going to have to put them on the spot, and make them think fast," said Sorenson with a laugh. "Most people don't have to come up with an answer to any question in a hurry. So they don't train their minds to do it. I've been on the spot with some very tough guys much more often than I like to think about. You learn to think fast and well, or you may not wake up the next morning.

"You train your men with a routine, check for fingerprints, look for hairs and fibers, talk to the neighbors. This is all good, and you get a lot of good information this way. But it teaches your men to ask the routine questions, not the odd questions.

"There's a silly joke about the police responding to a bank robbery. They search the bank, but they can't find the robbers. Finally the detective in charge says, 'How could they be gone, we've blocked all the exits' and this patrolman says 'Maybe they went out an entrance.' Sometimes you have to turn the question inside out to get the answer."

"So now we want a rich Albanian who was somewhere else in 2010," said Paul.

"Or the other options, one who changed his name perhaps," said Sorenson. "Or, even worse, one who was counted here in 2010, but who's not marked down as Albanian. My great-grandfather came to America from Norway, but in 1920 he was living with a bunch of Swedish families in a big apartment building. The census taker was lazy and put everybody down as Swedish. Great-granddad was furious when he saw the tally sheet, but the surveyor wouldn't change it. Maybe something similar happened here."

"We had just a dozen names," said Mahoney, "and now we have the whole county again. We're going backward. I'm not blaming you, Mr. Sorenson. You are actually doing us a unpleasant favor by poking all these holes in our theories. But we were hoping that you could do some positive help, as well."

"Have you checked with banks and brokerage houses for large withdrawals in 2013?" asked Sorenson. "If he paid a million dollars for the jewels, he must have gotten that money from somewhere. Some of my clients make very large payments, and they don't have that much cash just lying around. I get called about making the delivery, but I have to wait until they get the cash from wherever they have it.

"Mr. Stevens said it took a few days for the buyer to get the money together. So it probably wasn't sitting in a safe deposit box. Withdrawing the money from a bank or a brokerage would take a few days, because even banks don't normally have a million dollars just lying around. And if he had to sell stocks to get the money, the brokerage house wouldn't pay him until the stocks cleared. It's a large amount of money, there must be records."

"We already checked all the banks and brokerage houses in Berwyn," said Mahoney, "that's part of the routine. You know that."

"Yes, but did you check all the banks and brokerages in Chicago?" said Sorenson, "or Cook County? The loot was hidden in Berwyn, and it was found in Berwyn. But Mr. Stevens said he met the buyer in Chicago. I think you need to spread your net a little wider. And look for anyone, of any name or presumed nationality, taking out a million dollars in July of 2013. This is what you do best. You had the right idea, you just didn't think widely enough."

"Paul, I hate to interrupt you, but I just got a call from Stevens," said Detective Feltz. "He says he heard about Roscoe's run-in with the Miami cops and he's scared. He says he's going on vacation for a few days, but he won't say where he's going. Should we try to stop him?"

"He lives in Chicago," said Paul, "so we really don't have the legal authority to stop him. We could ask the Chicago police to do it, but even they will have a problem. We don't have a warrant for his arrest. We could hold him as a material witness, but Chicago can't – it's not their case. Tell him to stay in touch with us, and let him go. I want him willing to cooperate once we get Roscoe. Unhappy witnesses are a pain in the butt."

"There's an advantage for us if he goes on vacation," said Mahoney. "If everything goes wrong and Roscoe gets back here and finds out about Stevens, Roscoe can't do anything without Stevens. He has to ask Stevens about the buyer, just the same as we did. If Stevens isn't here, Roscoe is stuck."

"You're right, Sam," said Paul, "we know what Stevens knows and still can't find the buyer. Roscoe will have even more trouble without Stevens' information. Let him go, Mike, just make sure he keeps in touch."

***

Sorenson had been more careful about his bus rides home. Roscoe Queen may have taken his gang with him to Florida, but he might still have eyes looking around, hoping to see something that Mr. Queen would pay for. After all, someone had spotted him at Melissa's place.

Sorenson had told Mahoney and Radcliffe the truth about thinking well on his feet. But he hadn't told them the whole truth about his quick suggestion. He had spent his long hours of forced isolation thinking about the mysterious buyer. He was trying to get a feel for who the man might be, and how he might behave.

I've known many rich men with odd, and often expensive, hobbies and interests. Some had prized possessions, trophies, and treasures that they valued above almost anything. Other people might think these things of more limited value, but to the fanatic they were everything. He would protect them, perhaps by locking them up in a vault. But he might want to display his trophies, to show off to his friends, to delight himself by seeing them every day, like the guy with the Elvis jumpsuit. Protection and display were contradictory desires.

The man who bought the jewels – what was his intention in owning the crown, scepter and orb? Just to own them, for personal bragging rights, but keeping them hidden from the world? Possible, but most men would want to brag about such a treasure, show it off, telling some facile lie to explain how it ended up in their possession.

It's very unlikely that the treasure had been placed in a safe deposit box from the beginning. Almost certainly the man would have wanted to display it at home, either for just himself, or for his friends. His friends. He most likely has some Albanian friends, men he met here, or who had come with him from the old country. Maybe the police should look for non-rich Albanians, men who might know a rich friend who has a special treasure.

Detective Mahoney had said there were a few thousand people of Albanian ancestry in the Chicago area. How many could the buyer know? No, how many could know the buyer? He might personally know dozens, or even one or two hundred, but all of them might know him, if he was prominent in the community. No movie star personally knew a fraction of the people who knew her.

Thousands of people, scattered over who knew how many suburbs, and probably not in the nice tight ethnic neighborhoods immigrants formed a century earlier. Even with lots of manpower, the police would have trouble finding anyone who knows about the buyer. And what if they were tight-lipped? Some immigrants preferred not to work with the police against their compatriots. They came from a formerly Communist country – could they distinguish between police and secret police?

They might well know that the jewels had been in a museum, and are therefore stolen. Rather than give evidence against a rich fellow Albanian, they might say nothing to the police. Even if one man did say something, another might tip off the buyer. He could then hide the jewels, and show an innocent and empty house to the investigators.

None of this was going to help find the buyer. If the police could find the man who took out a million dollars from his bank, or wherever, that would settle the matter. And that is probably going to be faster than looking for an Albanian fink. But today is Sunday, and even an aggressive police department won't be able to get a banker or a stock broker to come in and open the office today.

So Monday the police start calling around to all the financial big shots, looking for a serious withdrawal five years ago. It might still be on their minds – a million bucks is still big money, and providing it in a hurry makes it more memorable.

Monday is also the first of October. I have three clients who will want me to deliver money to landlords and mistresses. I had hoped the case would have been wrapped up by now. At the very least, Mr. Queen and his gang should have been arrested. How long would it take them to return from Florida? Mr. Queen does not know my clients, or my schedule, so it might be safe enough to run my errands tomorrow. I certainly can't afford to offend these clients by not showing up.

Sorenson looked at his watch. It told him what his stomach had been suggesting for quite a while, it was late and time for dinner. A careful stroll down to the Moravian House Restaurant, a peaceful meal of Czech duck, dumplings and red cabbage, washed down with Krusovice dark, and another careful stroll home. No unexpected sightings on the street, or abnormally curious people. Wonderful.

Chapter Seventeen

The warm weather of late September was over, blown out of town by a cold north wind. October began on a cooler than usual note, windy and drizzly. People who had gotten used to sleeping with the windows open in late September, woke up cold, and grumbled. Restaurants with sidewalk tables were bringing them in for storage until next spring. People were putting their light jackets into the back of their closets and re-discovering their sweaters.

Zef wasn't concerned about the change in the weather. His apartment was always comfortable, summer and winter. He traveled by taxi all over the city, and had to be out in the elements only long enough to go from door to cab to door. His wife wanted him to exercise more, but even that could be done indoors at the health club. *Life is so easy and comfortable when one is rich,* he thought.

But this morning there was uneasiness and discomfort. Last night Ajola had helped him wrap the Crown Jewels. He had sometimes received items packaged with bubble wrap, and decided that this would be the best protection for the jewels. But he had no idea where he could buy it. America was too full of wonderful and amazing things – where might such a thing be sold? He had gone out Sunday afternoon and asked people in stores near his apartment. Finally someone pointed him to a store that sold bubble wrap.

He had taken the crown from its shelf first and held it carefully as Ajola wrapped the material around it. It was difficult to wrap the bubbled plastic around the goat's horns on top of the crown. She used a strip of Scotch tape to hold it in place, and then wrapped more around the base of the helmet. She then balled up some more wrap and stuffed it into the hollow of the crown. It looked grotesque and misshapen, but it was protected.

The orb was hard to wrap because it was spherical with a two-headed eagle on top. They ended up wrapping the material around and around the orb, swaddling it in bubble-wrap. The scepter was much easier to wrap, a two foot long staff with another eagle at the head. They just had to roll it in the bubble-wrap and they were done.

He went online to his bank's website and followed the links to the page about safe deposit boxes. He searched for the description of the box he had rented, and checked its dimensions. Ajola measured the size of the Crown, Orb and Scepter. It would fit, just barely. It took only a few minutes more to pack them into a suitcase.

Ajola had worried when he told her about the villainous men who were searching for the Crown Jewels. She was afraid they would kidnap and kill them as they had the policewoman and tried to do to the other man in Florida. Zef assured her that the jewels would be safely locked away in his safe deposit box, protected from any thieves.

And they would go on a vacation to Albania for a few weeks. They would visit their relatives and old friends, and tell them stories of their success in America. And they would be safe from these brigands. The American police were very good, and would soon arrest these men, and they could come home safely. She had been mollified by his reassurances, and used his computer to book them a flight on Tuesday.

But now, on Monday morning, Zef did not feel quite so certain about their future. *I can store the jewels safely away, and we would be safe across the ocean. But what about after we came back. The thieves would be under arrest, and therefore no threat. I'm not worried about that. But what about the jewels themselves? Will the police find out that I have them? Can I hide them from the police?*

I bought them fairly and honestly, and for a large sum of money. True, I have no bill of sale, no proof that I have a legal right to own them. No proof that the nameless man I bought them from had any right to them, either. Yes, I had often seen them in the museum, but I did not steal them myself, and did not really know if he had stolen them. That man did not look like the sort of man who would have such a treasure, but perhaps he had found it somewhere. I have a right to own these jewels, but would the police see things the same way?

Maybe they won't learn that I have the Crown Jewels. If they didn't know, then I can return from my vacation and retrieve the jewels from the vault. They could once again take their proper place in my shrine to my native land.

Zef picked up the suitcase and left his apartment for the short ride to his bank. He walked casually through the bank's lobby, noticing that no one was looking at him. For some reason, this reassured him. *If no one sees me, I'm not here, and I'm not hiding something in the vault.*

The young lady at the desk by the safe deposit vault was very cheerful this morning, but then, he had never seen her not being cheerful. That was why he liked this bank. They were very business-like, and also very friendly. It was not always the case with businesses, and it was pleasant that this bank should have both qualities. The friendliness was not essential, of course, but it made life a little more enjoyable. In a way, it reminded him of his village in Albania, where everyone knew everyone else, and they were all friends, if not family.

He signed in and the woman took his key from him as she led him into the vault. He had rented one of the largest boxes in the vault years ago. He hadn't really needed such a large box at the time, but thought it might be handy sometime. And he was rich and should have the largest of everything. It had been perfect to store his wife's anniversary present two years ago. And now it was just large enough for the Crown Jewels.

The woman removed the box from its place on the lowest level of boxes, and placed it on a table in a side cubicle. When she left, he opened the box and looked in.   Lots of papers, stock certificates, bonds, Ajola's best jewelry, but still plenty of room for the Crown Jewels.

He opened the suitcase and removed the crown carefully. He set it gently into the safe deposit box, laying it on its back, the goat horns resting on the bottom of the box. The orb just fit in at the front of the box, keeping the crown from sliding forward. The scepter was long, almost too long for the box, but he managed to put the base of the scepter in at the back bottom corner of the box and run it at an angle to the top of the box.

He closed the safe deposit box and told the young woman that he was finished with it. She placed it back in its hole, and returned his key to him. She must have noticed the difference in its weight, but she gave no sign that she had. He thanked her and left, smiling at having protected his treasure.

***

Sorenson opened his closet door and looked at the clothes inside. His back-up apartment did not have as good a selection of clothes as his regular one, and that was a problem today. He had to meet three rich men, looking respectable and business-like.   The suit he had been wearing when he had arrived here on Wednesday was getting wrinkled. The only other suit he had here was just a suit, not one that would convey the image he needed today.

But if the streets were safe enough to run errands for his clients, they were safe enough to go to his other apartment and get a nicer suit. Outside, he caught a bus and rode west for several blocks, got off and took another bus north. Two more buses brought him to within a block of his main apartment. A brisk walk brought him to his door and he went inside.

He changed his clothes and then packed some fresh clothes in a small suitcase. He'd have to come back for that later, but he didn't know how long he was going to have to live elsewhere. He looked out the window at his car, parked on the street below. He normally used it to run these errands, but it was too easy for someone to follow. Someone might be watching. Best to not take chances, taxis would be safe today and he didn't have to park them.

***

"Mr. John Smith to see Mr. Venucci," Sorenson told the receptionist. He never had an appointment with any of his clients, but he never had to wait very long. Occasionally, one might really be in conference, but most were able to slip away for the few minutes it took to pass three envelopes to Mr. Smith.

Two minutes later, the receptionist opened the door to Mr. Venucci's office and Mr. Smith walked in. The two men exchanged the usual pleasantries, and Mr. Venucci gave Mr. Smith a handshake and three envelopes.

"You're in luck this month," said Mr. Venucci, "you get a raise. The landlord raised the rent, so your fee is a bit more."

"Thanks for being honest about that," Mr. Smith said. "Some men would have tried to stiff me on that, figuring I wouldn't find out. I appreciate your fair play."

Sorenson found another cab without any trouble, and told the driver to take him to the Royal Arms Apartments. He asked the driver to wait, with the meter running. Drivers liked that, as long as their fare came out again.

Sorenson rang the bell for apartment 412, and was buzzed in. He took the elevator up to the fourth floor and walked down the corridor. As he approached number 412, the door opened, and a cute blonde with large breasts and a short skirt looked out at him.

"Right on time, Smitty," said the blonde, "I like that in a delivery man. Want to come in and get a nice warm thank you from me? Joe needn't know about it."

"There's your envelope," said Mr. Smith. "I appreciate the offer of hospitality, but you know my answer. It's the same answer I always give you. If Mr. Venucci ever did find out, I would lose a very profitable job, and so, probably, would you. We could both find other employers, but who needs the hassle? Besides, I have a taxi waiting."

Sorenson tipped his hat and said good-bye, sighing with relief as the door closed behind him.

***

"Mr. John Smith to see Mr. Watson," Sorenson told the receptionist. There was no wait to see Mr. Watson, who greeted him rather glumly.

"I, uh, I've got the money here, as agreed," said Mr. Watson. "But I'd like to discuss our arrangement, if you don't mind. I know I agreed to pay you 10 percent of the money you deliver, but it's getting to be a bit expensive for me. The girl wants more, and business is getting tight right now. Is there any way we can cut back your fee?"

"Sure, you can eliminate it entirely," said Mr. Smith. "You just have to make the payments in person yourself. You hired me to make the deliveries for you. My standard fee for this is 10 percent. If you make the payments yourself, you save my fee. If you don't want to make the payments yourself, you can try to find someone else to do it for you, and hope he charges less. Or you can mail the cash to the landlord and the girl.

"I don't like losing clients, but I also don't like taking a cut in pay. I do this to save you the bother and the embarrassment of doing it yourself. If I let you haggle over my fee, pretty soon I wind up making nothing, because there is no bottom limit except nothing.

"I don't give advice to my clients on how to handle their personal lives. They wouldn't take it anyway. But your options are to get a less expensive girlfriend, which you probably don't want to do. Or find her a cheaper apartment, which she certainly won't like. Or run your own errands. Or pay me. Your choice."

"Okay, okay," said Mr. Watson, "I'm sorry for coming off stingy. My wife wants us to cut back on our expenses until the business picks up. If she knew how much I pay for Helen, she'd blow a fuse. And I'm not getting rid of Helen, she's too good. Here's the money. Don't worry, it's all there."

Another cab took him to a smaller, newer apartment building, one with a marble exterior that shouted "expensive" to the world. The woman in apartment 211 was also obviously expensive, but she didn't shout it to the world.

"Oh, Mr. Smith," she said, opening her door, "please come in. Would you like a cup of coffee? No, you're always in a hurry to go somewhere else, aren't you?"

"That's right," said Mr. Smith, "I have lots of errands to run, and only so many hours in a day. Here's your envelope. Have a nice day."

Sorenson left the apartment thinking how differently he treated the two women. He hadn't even set foot inside the blonde's apartment. He had done that once, and had spent fifteen minutes trying to get out of her clutches. Mr. Venucci needed to visit her more often. But he had no objection to entering Helen's apartment. She knew which side her bread was buttered on, and would never risk her position with him. And she also looked on him as an underling, a paid errand boy, hardly worth paying any attention to. And that suited him just fine.

***

"Mr. John Smith to see Mr. Costello," Sorenson told the receptionist. He took a seat, because Mr. Costello was always a busy man. He didn't fake it, the way some people did, he really was busy the first of every month. Other days might be slow, but never the first. The door to the inner office opened abruptly, spilling out a half dozen men and women who rushed off to other offices. A tall man inside peered out and waved Sorenson in.

"Sorry to keep you waiting, Mr. Smith," said Mr. Costello, "but you know what my days are like at the start of the month. You should come back next week, maybe Wednesday, the tenth. I'd like to sit down and chat with you about things. I've got a few irons in the fire that you might be able to help me with. Meanwhile, here's this month's envelopes."

"Thank you," said Mr. Smith, "and I will try to make it next week. This week is likely to be very busy for me, but I think I can be free next Wednesday."

Mr. Costello's mistress was Jill, a girl whom Sorenson had once arranged as a one-time fling for Mr. Costello. He had enjoyed her so much he took her on as a full-time mistress, in a very nice, and expensive apartment in a Lake Shore Drive high rise.

The doorman let Mr. Smith in, and phoned up to let Jill know she had a visitor. The doorman opened the inner door, and Sorenson went through to the elevator. As he waited, a foreign looking man in a very nice suit came in carrying a suitcase, chatted briefly with the doorman, and joined him at the elevator.

Sorenson was surprised that they were both going to the same floor, and even more surprised that the stranger was following him down the corridor. The other man stopped one door short of Sorenson's destination and went into that apartment. Jill opened her door and asked Sorenson in.

"Here's your envelope, Jill," said Mr. Smith. "I just had the oddest experience. A man entered the lobby just after I got here. He waited with me for the elevator, got off on this floor, and just went into the apartment next door. I thought he was following me for some reason until he went in."

"Oh, that's Mr. Tanush," said Jill. "He's a foreigner, but he's all right. Oh, but that's an odd thing, too, isn't it? I just saw on the news about this big jewel robbery, all about the Albanian Crown Jewels, and all that. And guess what, Mr. Tanush is Albanian. Small world, huh?"

"Smaller than you can ever imagine," said Mr. Smith, thoughtfully. "I'd like to chat, Jill, but I've got some errands to run."

***

First things first. Sorenson headed for the two realty companies that handled the apartments for the three women. He waited while they counted the cash payments, and politely declined the receipts they offered him. His clients didn't want proof of their indiscretions for their wives to find.

He took a taxi to his bank next. He wanted to get today's pay deposited before he did anything else. He might have to go down some more dark alleys later. And, despite his belief in the safety of alleys, it was better to do that while not carrying large amounts of cash.

Another cab took him, finally, to the Berwyn Police Department. It was late in the afternoon, and he hoped to find both Mahoney and Paul Radcliffe on duty.   The desk sergeant phoned the detective bureau and Mahoney came out to the lobby to meet him.

"You'll never guess," said Mahoney, "we've got the buyer."

"So have I," said Sorenson.

"Zef Tanush," they said in unison.

"How could you possibly know this?" asked Mahoney in bewilderment. "We had to check with seven different banks and four different brokers to find him. You told us today was your day for paying off mistresses. How could you do it?   How could you fit it into your schedule, even?"

"My last stop was his next-door neighbor," said Sorenson. "She saw the news from Miami about the robbery. She mentioned how odd it was that the stolen jewels were Albanian, and so was the guy next door. And you know I don't believe in coincidences."

"I'll be damned," said Mahoney. "You are the luckiest guy I've ever known. You just happen to drop in next door to a guy we've been looking for. Just like that."

"Probably half of what I've told you all along was the result of luck," said Sorenson. "But, you have proof, I only had a suspicion. You could only hope to talk to him with what I learned. You found the withdrawal – that lets you get a search warrant. You did better than I did."

"True," said Mahoney, "but I'm not home free. I can't get a search warrant – Tanush lives in Chicago. I have to get the Cook County States Attorney to write up a request for a warrant, and then get some Chicago cops to serve it. I'll get to come along, since we cooperate, but they have to do any searching and seizing, or arresting. I've already sent in the request for a warrant, and that should be done by tomorrow morning.

"The museum robbery was nine years ago and it is still on the books as unsolved. The statute of limitations is 7 years for felony grand theft, but not if the criminal flees the state. Roscoe fled after the Third City Bank job, which was right after the museum burglary. So the clock started ticking on him again when he came back to Illinois last week. The same goes for the stolen property, maybe. I'm not a lawyer. The states attorney will figure that one out."

"Wait, only 'maybe' for the stolen property?" asked Sorenson. "That's all you can get Tanush for. If it's 'maybe' can you even get a search warrant? He didn't steal the jewels, he only bought them."

"That's true enough," said Mahoney, "and if the statute of limitations has run out, he's clear and we can't get a warrant or find the jewels. Stevens is probably clear because he sold the jewels long enough ago. Well, we still can arrest Roscoe for the burglary, the Third City Bank job, killing Peterson and Whitey, kidnapping and beating Phyllis – oh, the list just goes on and on.

"I think that the states attorney will be so happy to get Roscoe, Stevens will walk, and maybe even Tanush. The jewels will have to go back to the museum, obviously, regardless of the statute of limitations. This is the nice thing about being a cop – I don't have to puzzle out the legalisms, I just have to arrest people."

"Lucky you," laughed Sorenson. "But you haven't said how you're going to arrest Mr. Queen. He's still out there somewhere, coming back to Berwyn, you think. Do you expect him to be so frustrated with failing to find the jewels that he'll just turn himself in?"

"No, that would be too easy," said Mahoney. "If criminals did that I wouldn't have a job. They don't give awards to cops who get the easy arrests. But I've got an idea for getting Roscoe that should work with only a little bit of risk. Roscoe knows that Falkenberg didn't have the jewels, and that the Radcliffes don't have them. That leaves Hoover and Rodriguez.

"Rodriguez is living and working in Waukegan now, I only found him because his parole officer is still here. We couldn't get an address for him earlier, because he just moved there. That means Roscoe won't be able to find him. And he's not a likely candidate for the guy who sold the jewels since he went bust.

"Hoover is right here in town, and easy to find. Roscoe can find him without too much effort, and will. We're going to put on a little stage show for his benefit. And I will play the part of Hoover in this performance. Roscoe doesn't know Hoover from Adam, and he doesn't know me, either. Any man standing in Hoover's office or home will look like Hoover to Roscoe. We know what Roscoe looks like. He comes in, we grab him, end of story."

"What if he tries to grab you on the road to Hoover's office?" asked Sorenson.

"I told you once, I'm not dumb," said Mahoney. "I'll have some boys in unmarked cars nearby at all times. Sergeant Markham did such a nice job saving your life last week that I've given him the job of ramming any car that tries to force me off the road."

"It sounds as though you have it all planned out," said Sorenson, "I just hope for your sake that the plan works."

"Yeah, so do I," answered Mahoney.

***

"We've got to find a better way to go on the run," said Roscoe. "Two days coming back was just as bad as one day going down. And yes, Hernando, this van is more comfortable than the other one, but not for such a long trip. Do you remember where that closed bar was, Louie? Let's get back there and plan tomorrow out."

Twenty minutes later in the dilapidated bar, with the extension cord stealing electricity from the shop next door, Roscoe looked his gang over. They were all tired from the two long trips over one weekend. He hoped that they could be rested enough to grab Hoover in the morning. He didn't want to waste any more time trying to get the jewels.

"Louie, you're out on this," said Roscoe, "the cops around here know you. If they've got somebody watching Hoover, they'll spot you in an instant. And all the cops everywhere know you work for me. Cowboy,

you're new around here, do you want to make the grab? You're the
biggest of the bunch, and your dorky jacket does look all right."

"Sure, boss," said Cowboy, "just tell me what to do, and I'll do it."

"You just go into his office," said Roscoe, "and ask for Mr. Hoover.
Just like that, Mr. Hoover, nice and polite like, Mister Hoover. When they
point him out to you, just punch him, grab him, and run out the door with
him. We'll be there with this van. Toss him in, climb in yourself, and
we're off."

"That's easy enough, boss," said Cowboy, "I'll be nice and polite to
Mr. Hoover. I'll even punch him nice and polite."

Chapter Eighteen

"I apologize again for the inconvenience," said Mahoney at seven on Tuesday morning, "but as I told you last night on the phone, we think you might be in danger from these criminals. They made an attempt in Florida to kidnap the man you bought that house from. We think they may try to kidnap you as well.

"The city will put you up in hotel for the next few days. You will both be safely out of the way. We will have detectives posing as you here, and at your office, sir. And you can continue to run your business by phone or computer. I know it's not perfect, but we want to protect you and to capture these crooks."

"I have an important meeting with a client this afternoon," complained Mr. Hoover. "It can't be changed at this late hour. And it really can't be done over the phone."

"Does your client actually need to be on your premises for this meeting?" asked Mahoney. "I mean, can you meet with him somewhere else? And what time is the meeting?"

"Well, yes, I suppose so," said Mr. Hoover. "The meeting is set for three o'clock. What do you have in mind?"

"We've picked a nice hotel with a business center," said Mahoney. "They have a couple of private conference rooms, and we can arrange to borrow one of them for a few hours. Your staff people can bring what they need over earlier, and you'll just have to go downstairs. Will that work for you?"

"Yes, that would do," said Mr. Hoover. "It's a lot more James-Bond-like than I care for, but if you insist, I'll do it."

"Thank you, sir," said Mahoney. "These are dangerous men, and I don't want to risk your life."

Mrs. Hoover and a policewoman came out of the bedroom with two small suitcases. The policewoman took them out to the Hoover's car.

"I wanted to marry you, Dennis," said Grace Hoover with a grin, "because you had the drive and determination to make yourself rich. My mother wanted me to marry Larry Holborn because he was already rich. She said it would avoid a lot of hassle. She was right."

"How much less hassle was Larry's bankruptcy, do you suppose?" asked Dennis, grinning back at his wife. "I don't like this either, dear, but I don't want you to be attacked by thugs, and I certainly don't want to be kidnapped myself. The polite but insistent detective says it is for our own good, and that he will take care of us. Think of him as a doctor giving us an injection. It only hurts for a little while."

The policewoman came back into the house and escorted the Hoovers to the car. She drove them off with an unmarked car following them to the hotel. No one showed any interest in their leaving, or in their trip.

"Okay, the Hoovers are safe now," said Mahoney. "Ella, you are going to play Mrs. Hoover here in their house. Keep the garage closed, so no one will sneak in that way. Leave the drapes open and the blinds up. Roscoe and his gang don't know what either Hoover looks like, so you'll do just fine. Read the newspaper, watch TV, cook some food. Do house-wifey things. Pete, you're just here to back Ella up if there's any trouble. You need to stay out of sight, but pay attention to any commotion.

"Markham, have you got that Expedition battering ram ready for another crash? Then, lets go. I've got to be at Hoover's office by eight."

***

"Just take it nice and easy," said Roscoe to Cowboy, "you're just a customer, or a buyer, or a salesman. Someone a place like this expects to walk in the door. When they point out Hoover to you, grab him and hustle him out. Hernando, I want you to drive the van – you did a good job in Miami. Leroy, the cops here don't know you either. I want to drop you off first, a block away from Hoover's business. Walk around the block, and the block opposite his place. Look for cops, unmarked squads, anything that says 'police trap.' When you get back to the van, we'll decide if we go in.

"If the cops are waiting, we'll try to get him at lunch time, or on the way home. If we have to, we'll wait until tonight to grab him in bed. If the cops aren't there, we go in as planned. Louie, you and me will be waiting in the van for Cowboy and Hoover. Get your gun out, just in case.

Everybody understand the plan? Good. Leroy, here's where you get out. Around the block to the left, then to the right. Go on."

Leroy stepped out of the van and strolled casually down the sidewalk. He had no jacket on and found it rather chilly. It was still only nine in the morning in early October. The weather had been fine here last week, and he hadn't thought to bring a jacket to Miami. But his jacket was still at Biff Tollandson's bar, left behind by accident when Biff tossed them out.

As he walked along the street, Leroy glanced around discreetly, not looking directly at anything, but only toward it. He was watching for cars parked along the street with men just sitting in them, for men standing around looking at the street more than at each other, for pedestrians who looked too tough and cop-like for the neighborhood. He wasn't seeing any signs of police activity so far. Very little activity of any type, in fact. A few people hurrying along the sidewalk, and a big van with a mechanic under it at a repair shop. There were lots of repair shops, and most had somebody under a car in front. He wondered why they bothered with the repair bays.

The blocks in Berwyn stretch out long north and south, so it took Leroy quite a while to finish going around the first block. That helped him, as most of the small groups of men he had seen earlier had moved elsewhere. Around the second block at last, and back to Cermak in front of Hoover's business. Still nothing to report. The sidewalks were still almost empty, and the mechanic was still poking around under the van. There was no sign of police anywhere. He hopped back into the van.

"All clear, Roscoe," he said as he got in. "Not a trace of a cop anywhere around here."

"Okay, boys, let's do it," said Roscoe. "Pull up there in front of Hoover's business, Hernando, and be ready to move as soon as Cowboy brings him out."

Despite his name, Cowboy was actually the best dressed member of the gang. Leroy liked a Dodgers jacket, now lost, having come from Los Angeles. Hernando favored a slick but garish green jacket. For some reason he thought it made him more attractive to women. Roscoe and Louie preferred black leather, the traditional garb of the hoodlums of their younger days. Cowboy wanted to look more refined, as he called it. He wore a dark blue blazer he had taken from a night club a year earlier. No one would mistake him for a proper business man, but he did not look like a thug, and that was the main thing.

He opened the door and went into an outer office crowded with desks and people working. He saw a door on the wall opposite him with a sign saying "Dennis Hoover." One of the desks was right by that door, and was occupied by a middle-aged woman in a woman's jacketed business suit. Cowboy walked up to the desk and told the woman seated there that he would like to see Mr. Hoover.

"Do you have an appointment?" asked Sergeant Joan Prchal, playing the role of receptionist for this production.

"No, I don't" said Cowboy, pleasantly, "but I would like to speak to him about a mutually profitable business venture." Cowboy had taken his speech from a movie he had seen recently, believing it to be the way real business men talked.

"I'll see if he's available," said Sergeant Prchal. Speaking into an intercom, she said, "Sir, there's a man here to see you."

After a muffled reply, she got up from her chair and opened the door to the inner office, and motioned Cowboy in. He went into the office and approached Mahoney, holding out his right hand for a handshake. He didn't notice that the receptionist was still holding the door open, and reaching under her jacket with one hand.

As he grabbed Mahoney's hand, Cowboy swung his left fist at Mahoney's face. To his surprise, Mahoney seemed to have expected the punch, and dodged back from it. Cowboy pulled Mahoney closer and swung again, this time aiming at Mahoney's stomach. He connected, knocking the wind out of Mahoney. He was just about to throw his victim over his shoulder when he felt a gun pressing against his back.

"Put your hands in the air," said Sergeant Prchal sternly, "you are under arrest."

Many things happened then all at once. Cowboy turned around abruptly, trying to push the gun away from his back, and knock the woman down. Mahoney, gasping for air, jumped for the turning Cowboy, trying to grab his arms. Patrolman Wozinski, also in civilian clothes, had been sitting by the front door. Seeing the action, and the van outside that

Cowboy had exited, he called on his radio to the backup team down the street.

The mechanic under the van jumped up, tapped on the driver's window of the van, and started running across the street. Sergeant Markham, crouched out of sight behind the steering wheel, sat up and hit the gas. He pulled out onto the street, driving fast toward Hoover's office and the van parked in front of it.

In the van, Roscoe and Louie, looking through the glass door to the office, saw the commotion inside. Roscoe, fearing the loss of his only link to the jewels, made a fateful, if rash, decision. He leaped out of the van and ran into the office. From his point of view, he had not seen Sergeant Prchal draw her gun on Cowboy, and he had not noticed Patrolman Wozinski by the door.

Mahoney, however, had seen Roscoe coming in with a drawn gun, and he tackled Cowboy. He pushed Cowboy and Sergeant Prchal to the floor, and threw himself on top of Cowboy. Wozinski, seeing no one behind Roscoe, rose from his desk, drew his own gun, and approached Roscoe from behind.

"Freeze! Drop the gun!" Wozinski shouted to Roscoe, as he put his gun to Roscoe's back.

Roscoe finally realized that he had rushed into a trap. He turned his head to look for Louie coming up behind him in support, and saw the van driving off. He and Cowboy were trapped, and he didn't know how many cops he was facing. He ducked his head and upper body down, and twisted around to confront Wozinski, but the patrolman took a step back and fired a shot at point blank range into Roscoe's shoulder.

The pain staggered Roscoe and made him pause, but only slowed him as he tried to grapple with the young policeman. But the pause gave Wozinski time to step back again for a second shot, this time into Roscoe's knee. Crying out in extreme pain, Roscoe fell to the floor, blood flowing freely from his leg.

In the inner office, Mahoney was keeping Cowboy pinned in place. Cowboy couldn't reach his own gun so he tried to throw Mahoney off of him. But Sergeant Prchal, also on the floor, had recovered from her fall faster, and once more pointed her gun at Cowboy. He looked at her and heard the gunfire and the screams from the front office. It all told him the game was up. He flattened himself on the floor and surrendered.

Meanwhile, Louie watched Roscoe jump out of the van and storm into the office. He realized what the commotion inside had meant, what Roscoe had not recognized, that this was a trap, and they were all about to be caught. He tried to stop Roscoe, but failed. So he slammed the sliding door of the van and told Hernando to get them out of there at once.

Hernando floored the gas pedal and the van started off down the street, but a large Ford SUV suddenly slammed into them head on. Hernando was strapped into his seat belt, but the others weren't and were thrown around by the impact. Leroy, in the front passenger seat, would have cracked his head against the windshield if the airbag hadn't deployed. Even so, he was dazed for a minute.

Louie was half seated on the edge of the middle seat of the van, leaning forward and looking out the side of the van to see if Roscoe had escaped. He was thrown backward into the third row of seats by the force of the crash, and banged his head hard against the back seat.

Sergeant Markham, shaken but unhurt, undid his seat belt and sprang from the SUV. The fake mechanic was already standing at the driver's door, holding a gun on Hernando. Markham opened the passenger door and pulled Leroy from the van before he could offer any opposition. Another policeman, running across from the repair shop also, opened the sliding side door, and made Louie give up his gun.

Mahoney handcuffed Cowboy while Sergeant Prchal kept her gun on him, then he turned the new prisoner over to her. He called the station to report his success. He could see the escape vehicle stopped outside, swarming with cops. He almost laughed as he told Paul and the chief the good news.

Mahoney came out of the building, still rubbing his stomach, but smiling at a highly successful sting operation. Five dangerous criminals captured, only one of them wounded, but not fatally. No police injuries (his stomach didn't count), and no civilians injured, either. They had been scared, especially when the gun fight started. But not one of them had been hurt, and they had a wonderful story to tell over dinner tonight.

Regular squads arrived in large numbers from both directions, sirens blaring, lights flashing, tires squealing. Hernando was pulled from the van and searched. Two guns were taken from him before he was handcuffed and placed next to Leroy. Louie and Cowboy soon joined them alongside the squads. A second, more thorough, search turned up two switchblade knives and a small palm gun. The men were then bundled into the squads for transport back to the station for booking.

An ambulance arrived last, and its crew went into the office to tend to Roscoe. They put a tourniquet around his leg to slow the bleeding from his shattered knee. Then they strapped him onto a body board and picked him up. A few steps brought them back out to the ambulance, and they put Roscoe in and took him away, still moaning loudly in pain.

The street slowly returned to normal as the ambulance and squads departed. Two squads remained, waiting for Mahoney and his assistants. Prchal and Wozinski worked to calm down the office staff, asking if any of them wanted to speak to a trauma counselor. Someone recovered presence of mind enough to find a bucket of water and a mop. A still jittery man said, "Let me do that, I need to do something simple and mindless to calm myself down." In a few minutes all traces of Roscoe's blood were cleaned up.

Once the shooting started, a great many people had come running out to see what was happening. No one seemed to think that shooting might involve stray bullets flying through the neighborhood. They stayed to watch the arrests and the removal of the criminals, and to discuss what they had seen. Eventually, the excitement died away, and they went back to their normal lives.

Once he had seen the prisoners on their way to the police station, Mahoney had called Mr. Hoover.

"Mr. Hoover, this is Detective Mahoney. Everything went according to our plan, and Roscoe and his entire gang are now in police custody. You and your wife are now totally safe. I'm sending a car to pick you up to come here. We'll drive your wife home, too.

"There was a small bit of fighting and shooting in your offices. No damage was done. None of your employees was injured, but I suspect many of them are very worked up. Actually, they mostly seem excited by what happened. Once your meeting is over this afternoon, you might want to give everyone the rest of the day off."

***

Mahoney wrote his report quickly. He always did. He knew what he had done, what the criminal had done, what else may have happened. He put the facts together in his head on the way back to the station almost every time. Then all he had to do was type it up, and he was a fast typist. His report, as always, was short and to the point. This happened, that happened, we succeeded, I failed. Success had to be shared, failure was always personal, even when it wasn't, especially when it wasn't.

Mahoney made one last phone call to Ralph Stevens.

"Mr. Stevens, this is Detective Mahoney. All is well here. The criminals have all been arrested, and it is safe for you to come home. I have no problem with you and your wife enjoying the pretty leaves back East if you still want to. We would like to talk to you when you return, but we may have some good news for you then."

The chief of police and the Radcliffes came in as he finished, the chief beaming with joy. He put his arm around Mahoney and slipped a small flask into his pocket.

"Congratulations, Mahoney," he said elatedly. "That's just for walking around, the whole new bottle will be delivered to your home tonight. I'm proud of you and your team. Five of the worst criminals we've had in Berwyn in a long time, captured with hardly any fuss. If I could promote you on my own authority, I would. But this will go down very well with the promotion board, very well. Test scores are one thing, but solid performance beats everything."

"Thank you, sir," said Mahoney. "I won't be modest and say it was nothing. It could have been a disaster, but everyone on the team did their bit exactly right. No one hesitated or fumbled. Wozinski was especially cool, with Roscoe Queen right in front of him. I hope he does well on the sergeants' examination next June – we can use more good men like that, and not just patrolling."

"Well, it's good to have so many crimes wrapped up all at once like this," said the chief. "We've been trying to find Roscoe for the Third City Bank job for years, and the murders of Peterson and McGraw, and your kidnapping, Phyllis. And the Albanian Crown Jewels robbery, too."

"We can't nail Roscoe for both Peterson and McGraw," said Paul. "They were shot with two different guns. I can believe that Roscoe killed McGraw. Maybe he thought Whitey had betrayed him somehow. But Peterson wouldn't let Roscoe get near him, so one of the newer gang members must have killed him. Most likely the one who hired him to begin with."

"And the jewels are going to be a tricky charge," said Mahoney. "We are fairly certain that Roscoe and his original gang did that robbery. But we have no proof. All we have is their knowledge of where the loot was hidden. And the only members of that gang that are left are Roscoe and Louie. Roscoe won't confess. Louie, he's a little smarter than Roscoe, and maybe he'll talk for a deal on his sentence. Maybe not, he's going to get a stiff sentence for the rest of his rap sheet anyway.

"Oh, I forgot the two guys who survived the Third City Bank job and got locked up. They would have been in on the Stiplitz robbery, too. Maybe they can be persuaded to testify against Roscoe. Offer them a little time off of their sentences. Not our job to worry about that anyway, chief, that's what states attorneys are for."

"And we haven't got the jewels yet, either," said Phyllis. "I went out with the warrant team from the Chicago PD, and our Albanian friend wasn't home. He left a message with the doorman to hold his mail for him while he's on vacation in Albania. I think we can recover the items when he comes back, but that is also going to be a job for the states attorney. How lucky can one man get?"

"Oh, cheer up," said the chief. "We got Roscoe Queen! We got the whole gang! The states attorney isn't stupid, and will be able to find a charge that fits each and every one of them. Once we get the last bits of paperwork done, I'm taking you all out to Luigi's Steak House. On me."

***

Sorenson tidied up his secondary apartment. He was a normally neat person, making his bed each morning, washing his dishes right after he ate, sweeping and dusting regularly. But a little disorder always crept in, and a little extra re-ordering left the apartment ready for its next use, in a week, or a month.

He returned his spare phone to its hiding place, and the money to its place under the drawer. He turned down the thermostat and closed the blinds. He removed the perishable food from the refrigerator and put it into a plastic bag. He put his dirty clothes, along with the food, in the small suitcase he had brought over yesterday and carried it out with him, down the stairs and onto a bus.

At his regular apartment, he picked up a week's worth of mail: his bank statement, a credit card offer, and an invitation to a high-finance seminar. The credit card offer and the invitation went into the trash. He would take the bank statement to his other secret apartment, the one where he kept his financial records. It wasn't really an apartment, just a rather small office. But he kept a cot and a couple of blankets there, just in case his other spare apartment was discovered.

He went out to the store and restocked his pantry and refrigerator. When he got home he looked at his watch. It was four in the afternoon. *One week. That's all it was, from beginning to end. A week ago, just now, I was entering an empty bar. What a god-awful week it was, too. For Peterson, dead because he didn't know what he knew. For the Radcliffes, burgled for something they didn't have. For Phyllis Radcliffe, kidnapped and beaten for not knowing what she couldn't know.*

I should quit this work, it's gotten too dangerous. No, that's not true. It was only dangerous this week because of Roscoe Queen. He's in jail, and won't be getting out ever again. Besides, how else can I support myself? I don't have any other skills, and I'm too old to learn some more legitimate trade.

Move somewhere else? Where? Any other place, I wouldn't know my way around the town, or the people. I know where the mine fields are here, and how they're arranged. Someplace else, I'd be blown up the first day. Besides, Marcy is here, and she won't move. And I'd miss her a lot if I moved. Now that this is over, I should give her a call. Maybe do dinner tonight.

It's actually a nice job. I don't have to work hard most of the time. I have easy hours, and can come and go as I please. I have to make nice to rich men who are sometimes unpleasant, but they pay me well. What was it the snob Pooh-bah said in The Mikado on taking a bribe? Ah yes,

"Another insult and, I think, a light one!" Only I don't get light insults, they are quite plump.

And I have made some nice friends with the Berwyn Police Department. They will listen to my questions when I need information, and they might give me some. They may do more than that. Detective Mahoney mentioned the possibility, and only the possibility, of my getting a reward out of all this chaos. For the return of the jewels, maybe, or the arrest of Roscoe Queen and his gang, or maybe not. It's always someone else's decision.

Sorenson's phone rang, interrupting his thoughts.

"Yes," he said, guardedly.

"Mr. Smith," said an unknown voice nervously, "I've been given your phone number by a mutual friend. He tells me that you do favors, or run errands......

EPILOGUE

The meetings lasted six days, though it seemed much longer to most of the people involved. Technically, it was longer, since the sessions rarely ended before eight in the evening, and once went on until ten. Only the first day and the last day were of a reasonable length, which was strange because those were the two days with the most people attending.

The Chicago Regional Office of Foreign Missions, a unit of the U.S. Department of State, served as the host for the meeting. On Monday morning its conference room filled with representatives of the U.S. State Department, the Republic of Albania, the Cook County States Attorney, the Illinois Attorney General, the U.S. Attorney General, the Chicago Police Department, the Berwyn Police Department, the Stiplitz Museum, Zef Tanush, and Ralph Stevens.

The State Department sent just one official, Mr. Thomas Hogan, as a sign of respect for and cooperation with the Albanians. The two police departments also sent just one person each, since the Cook County States Attorney would do all the talking for them. The two Attorneys General also sent only one lawyer each, since they were merely overseeing someone else's work.

The Cook County States Attorney was there in person, to present her official decisions on the various aspects of the matters at hand. She had three assistants to handle the paperwork and to remind her of any details she might forget.

The Stiplitz Museum sent its president, chief attorney and two deputy attorneys. They hoped to obtain the return of the Albanian Crown Jewels to their collection. Their briefcases bulged with legal citations supporting their position.

The Republic of Albania was represented by its ambassador to the United States, three lawyers and a translator. The translator was merely a precaution against possible misunderstandings. The ambassador and her lawyers all spoke English well.

Last of all were Zef Tanush and Ralph Stevens, their wives, and their lawyers, all of whom looked rather despondent and worried.

"Since the State Department is providing this room," said Mr. Hogan, "my colleagues in government have allowed me to play host, and so I welcome all of you here today. I will personally have little to say in your deliberations. I expect to do no more than to sign off on whatever agreement you jointly make. After speaking with some of you earlier, I think the best way to begin is to deal with the legal matters involving Mr. Tanush and Mr. Stevens. I give the floor to the Cook County States Attorney, Ms Wolfe."

"Thank you, Mr. Hogan," said Ms Wolfe. "Just over nine years ago, a gang of thieves broke into the Stiplitz Museum and stole a crested medieval helmet, an orb, and a staff, collectively known as the Albanian Crown Jewels. Thanks to the cooperation of Mr. Tanush, these items are now in the possession of my office. The rest of these meetings will be to determine who has the best claim to ownership. Today we will begin by clearing up the legal records.

"The men who stole these items from the museum have been arrested and await trial. They hid the jewels in a private house, where Mr. Stevens found them by accident. He sold them to Mr. Tanush. Mr. Stevens took the jewels without anyone's permission, which is theft. However, the home owner at the time did not know the jewels were there, did not know they were taken, and filed no complaint about the theft.

"He did not take the jewels from their rightful owner, although he admits he had no right to take them himself. His lawyer has already submitted a comment to me on the precise legal definition of theft. And I have to admit that his client will appear sympathetic to a jury, especially after this week's work. I have the original thieves to prosecute and see no benefit in trying Mr. Stevens. He was opportunistic, and wrong, but I would prefer not to try cases I can't win. Mr. Stevens, unless the state or federal attorneys general have any objection, you are free to go. There will be no charges placed against you, now or later."

"Oh, my goodness!" yelled Ralph Stevens. "Really? Oh, thank you, thank you, thank you! Oh, Alice, I'm free! We can go home!"

Ralph hugged and kissed his wife repeatedly. He shook his lawyer's hand and patted him on the back. They left the conference room elated and were halfway down the corridor when a thought struck him.

"They didn't say anything about the money. Do I get to keep it?
And with all those federal lawyers there, no one mentioned my taxes. Am
I still in trouble?"

"They didn't ask for the money," said his lawyer, "so I don't think
they want it. Tanush gave you the money, and he doesn't want it back, so
don't worry about that. As for your taxes, I don't know. No one
mentioned them, either. You will have a real problem if someone looks
into your tax returns. Hope no one does. And get a good tax lawyer, just
in case."

***

Back in the conference room, Ms Wolfe was addressing Mr. Tanush.
"You had been a frequent visitor and knew the crown and other objects
had been in the Stiplitz Museum. This makes it hard for you to claim that
you did not know when you bought them that they had been stolen.
However, the statute of limitations on receiving stolen property has run
out, but not for possession. However, you have cooperated with us fully
in returning the jewels. The Albanian ambassador has asked to say
something on your behalf, so I will hold off deciding your fate to hear her
speak. Madame Ambassador?"

"Thank you," said the ambassador. "As you have mentioned, there
are many questions about the ownership of these items which we will
argue about all week long, I am sure. But Mr Tanush has made that
discussion possible. Had he not purchased these items they might well
have disappeared into some private collection, never to be seen again.

"My country is pleased with his devotion to his old homeland and
love of its history.   His actions may not have been strictly legal, but he
acted not for personal profit, but from love of his country. My
government has instructed me to offer to Mr. Tanush the position of
honorary consul in Chicago. This title carries some minor duties, but no
diplomatic protection. However, I hope that you will take his native land's
pride in him into account in your decision."

"Thank you, Madame Ambassador," said Ms Wolfe, "I am happy to
do so. We had discussed this possibility, but I needed to know your
government would make the offer. I can hardly prosecute an honorary
consul, even without diplomatic immunity. Mr. Tanush, I am happy to

clear you, as well. You do understand that the jewels will stay in my possession until their final disposition is determined here. And that you will almost certainly not receive them."

"Yes, lady, Ms Wolfe," stuttered Zef. "I thank you for your compassion. I love my homeland, but I also love my new homeland, where justice is everywhere. Come, Ajola, we must go out and celebrate."

Out in the corridor, Zef turned to his lawyer and said, "You will join us in celebrating. And you are still 'on the clock' as you say. I still want to keep the Crown Jewels, and you must help me find a way to do this."

***

Mr. Hogan of the State Department adjourned the meeting for lunch. When they reconvened, the policemen were gone, as was Ms Wolfe, now represented by one deputy. The various government lawyers moved down to the far end of the table with Mr. Hogan. The rest of the table was now fully in the hands of the lawyers for the museum and Albania.

"When Albania became a kingdom in 1928," said the Ambassador, "we requested the return of the historic Albanian crown of Skanderbeg from Austria. They complied and we added an orb and scepter to complete the Crown Jewels. When Italy under Mussolini invaded Albania, the jewels were taken to Rome and later disappeared. Even under the communists, Albania never relinquished its claim to these jewels. So, we would ask that they be returned to us now."

"Thank you, Madame Ambassador," said George Stiplitz, "that was a very clear and concise account of the history of the Crown Jewels of Albania. When my father founded his museum after World War Two, he sought for many treasures of central European origin. He wanted a museum for the art and cultures that had been overrun by the Soviets. He was offered these items by a refugee in 1949, a man who had no idea of what they were, only that they were from eastern Europe.

"It took my father three years to learn what he had. By then, the communists were firmly in charge in Albania. He did ask if they wanted the jewels returned, but they rejected them as symbols of what they called their 'decadent past.' So he kept them and put them on display in his museum. He had paid for them, and the then-current Albanian government did not want them. I see no reason why we should not keep them. We will address Mr. Tanush's complaint and give them a more prominent display."

Such were the battle lines, and neither side was willing to yield an inch from their positions. Historic national pride was countered by historic national disdain. Possession was, or was not, the most important issue. International laws about the return of items looted in wartime roused the government officials at the other end of the table. But even they could not sway any opinions.

***

Saturday morning found most of the disputants at their places, looking dispirited and wrung out. The ambassador and Mr. Stiplitz arrived last, together, with smiles on their faces.

"Mr. Hogan," began the ambassador, "the Republic of Albania and the Stiplitz Museum have reached an agreement. And we owe it all to our new honorary consul. Mr. Tanush has offered to pay for the creation of a duplicate of the Crown Jewels. The originals will be returned to Albania, where they will be given a place of honor in the National Museum of History. The duplicates will be given to the Stiplitz Museum, which has already agreed to display them as they deserve. We have drawn up the official documents to authorize this, in English and Albanian, and would be pleased to have our signatures witnessed by yourself and these other officials."

***

"Ah, Zef, darling," said Ajola, "you were so clever to suggest making a copy of the crown. Now everyone is happy, and you are honored even more by Albania. And it is not so bad to go to the museum to see the jewels, is it?"

"What? Why should I go to the museum to see them?" said Zef. "I had the craftsman make two copies, and he will bring us our copy tomorrow. What is the use of my wealth if not to make us happy?"

***

"Mr. Ralph Stevens?" said the gray haired man at the door. "My name is Philip Walker. I'm with the Internal Revenue Service, and I'd like to talk to you if I may."

"Oh, no," moaned Ralph, "I was hoping you had forgotten all about me, or maybe never heard of me. Oh, well, I can't avoid it, I guess. Come on in."

"You were in the news quite a bit last month," said Mr. Walker, "and that made it hard to ignore you. I was given the task of looking into your previous tax records to determine if you had paid the tax on your million dollar windfall. As you know, you did not. I calculated the taxes, the penalties, and the combined interest, well, it's almost half a million dollars."

"Oh, god, I'm ruined," cried Ralph. "Is there anything I can do? Can I offer to pay in installments? Do I have to go to jail? Oh, god!"

"Let me finish, Mr. Stevens," said Mr. Walker. "I did not come here to arrest you. I came to give you this receipt, showing that your tax bill has been paid in full."

"Paid? Who paid?" asked Ralph. "I didn't pay. I couldn't pay. I can't pay. How, who, ..."

"Mr Stevens, I read all about this fascinating story when I was given your file," said Mr. Walker. "You're a guy who stumbled onto a pot of gold and kept it. You should have paid taxes on it, and you know that. I should put you away for tax evasion. I've done it to lots of people. But it doesn't really make me happy to ruin someone's life.

"I know how the system works, how the money is collected, and how the records are updated. The man who takes in your payment looks at your file only to see what you owe. If the check matches that amount, he marks the file 'paid in full' and that's it. The man who works on the file only needs to see that 'paid in full' note. He never sees the check. If the file is marked 'paid in full', a receipt gets printed off and sent to you. And here it is.

"Keep this in a safe place. No one should ever come here again about these taxes. If someone should come to see you, just show them this receipt. It is proof that you paid your taxes."

"But I didn't," said Ralph, "you know I didn't."

"Mr. Stevens," said Mr. Walker, "I have here an official government document which clearly states that you have paid your taxes in full. Would the government lie about a thing like that?"

"I, uh, I, what," mumbled Ralph, "I don't understand. What…? Why….?"

"Mr. Stevens," said Mr. Walker, "the government wants this money. It always wants money, and more money. The half million I should take from you will be spent in about four minutes, less time than we have talked already. It doesn't matter if it's spent well or foolishly, it goes so fast nobody notices.

"I have worked for the Internal Revenue Service for forty years. I have sent a lot of people to jail or financial ruin over those years. Some of these people have deserved this. Some others have not been guilty of anything more than carelessness or stupidity. It hurt sometimes to do this, but I always told myself it's just my job. But I'm retiring in two weeks, and it's Christmas time. I don't want to retire with a bad taste in my mouth. Here's your receipt. Don't tell anyone but your wife how you got this receipt, that would only cause trouble. Merry Christmas, and goodbye."

www.ingramcontent.com/pod-product-compliance
Lightning Source LLC
Chambersburg PA
CBHW060424130626
46555CB00005B/2206